SLICER

Earl Long

Writers Club Press
San Jose · New York · Lincoln · Shanghai

Slicer

Copyright © 2000 by Earl G. Long

This book may not be reproduced or distributed, in whole or in part, in print or by any other means without the written permission of the author.

ISBN: 0-595-08978-X

Published by Writers Club Press, an imprint of iUniverse.com, Inc.

For information address:
iUniverse.com, Inc.
620 North 48th Street
Suite 201
Lincoln, NE 68504-3467
www.iuniverse.com

URL: http://www.writersclub.com

For Shay, Jeremy and Albert Jr.

To Alexa Selph,
Lauri Young, Sue Anderson, Pam Wilkerson,
Carolyn James, Nora Day,
and Bill Murrain:
Thanks, thanks, and thanks.

1

He had been running so hard that even his thoughts were exhausted, coming in fragments: Going to die…got to keep running…faster…dunes on left…hide in grass…won't escape…going to die. No…not going to die.…Hell, no.

The voice from the figure running behind him spoke calmly, as if it had been floating, not racing to keep up with him. "There will only be a slight sting. I do not indulge in inflicting unnecessary pain. But there is nothing I can do to prevent your death. This is inevitable."

The man in front tried to force more speed from his legs. The voice behind him was calm and soothing, "You will make it to the foot of the dune, then I must kill you. It is getting late."

He tried to hate the voice; tried to force his anger; make himself stop and fight; but nothing. Just the helpless compulsion to run until he died. In the faint moonlight, the top of the dune offered a smooth, rounded comfort. A few feet more…just another second…large clump of tall grass on the left…dive to the ground…roll to the right…jump up and run to the left. He faltered for a second, and put his left hand out to stop his fall, felt a slight warmth across his throat, and suddenly he was free of the assassin.

He leaped high over the dunes, moving so quickly that his feet couldn't feel the ground; so fast, that the wind burned his face. Free...free. He was laughing loud and hard. "Shithead, can't touch me, now. Shithead," he was shouting to the shadow behind him. He had never been so happy, so untouchable.

The pursuer stepped over the body, and listened until the breath had stopped gurgling out of the severed trachea. He stepped back to avoid the stream of blood pumping out too rapidly for the sand to absorb before it spread into a dark halo around the corpse's head.

Then he walked away, paused, and looked up at the sky, breathed deeply for thirty seconds, and finally emptied his lungs with a slow woosh. He removed his shoes and slacks, and waded into the sea up to his ankles. Rinsed the blood from the ribbon-thin carbon-steel blade then plunged it repeatedly into the sand. He reached for a cord around his neck and pulled it up to reveal a black plastic sheath, inserted the knife, and slipped the sheath back under his shirt. He returned to the spot where he had left his pants, and brushed the water off his legs. He pulled his slacks back on and walked back the way he had run, keeping to the edge of the waves where his footprints would soon disappear.

Almost immediately, he began thinking of the geological events that had shaped the beach and the dunes, tried to identify the sounds of unseen animals rustling in the grass beyond the waves. Someday, the remains of the night things and everything else around him would be hundreds of feet under the sea. The dunes would be compressed into sandstone, then the immense sheets of rock would be pushed into the great furnace under the continental shelf to be recycled. When he opened the door of the car, the roof light did not come on. The panel lights were set too low to show his face clearly. He had to lean forward to read the time on the digital clock. Twelve thirty-four. The victim would not have remembered his face if he had survived anyway. But the assassin never took chances. He continued to think of geologic cataclysms and processes as he drove away. This made him think of the

Himalayas, but he pushed that thought away. He would reserve consideration of the Himalayas and its fossils for his next job.

He kept his speed exactly at three miles over the speed limit as he drove north to Savannah. He drove through the city until he found a gas station with several black customers. He walked up to the window and pushed three five-dollar notes under the window. "Fifteen…pump two," he said, keeping his eyes on the attendant's hands. He walked slowly to the gas pump, mouth pursed as if he were whistling. Nothing to make anyone want to look again. Six feet tall, close-cropped hair, black cotton tee-shirt, dark gray pants, black running shoes, no socks. No wristwatch or jewelry. Nothing special about his face, could be anybody. Just another black customer.

2

Four hours later, he was home in East Atlanta, with only a faint memory of what had happened earlier. A man had died, he knew that. He was involved. He knew that. He had done a job well, he knew that too. Later in the day, he would leave as soon as decently possible after his last class at Charteris University; he would drive to a pay telephone at Hartsfield Airport and call a bank in the Cayman Islands. He could probably get to the airport by three-thirty. He was already enjoying the female voice with the singing accent telling him that a deposit of one hundred thousand dollars had been made to his account. He would ask the voice to repeat the amount. Someday, he would visit the bank and ask to see the owner of the voice. A calm, efficient voice—like his; but warmer because she wanted to leave a good impression on the tape recorder monitoring all calls.

He took his shoes off on the steps of the small redbrick house with white trim, and rinsed his feet with the hose lying across the bed of petunias. In the bathroom, he threw the shoes into the tub and stepped in. He removed his clothes and reached into the cupboard under the washbasin for a plastic garbage bag. Put his discarded clothes and underwear into the bag and secured it with a wire tie. He adjusted the hot and cold taps until the water was almost unbearably hot, and scrubbed his entire body with ivory soap and a loofa sponge. He shampooed, rinsed and dabbed himself dry with a soft towel, because his skin burned from the hot water and rough scrubbing. He put on a terry-cloth robe and carried the soiled bag to the kitchen garbage bin.

He made himself a dinner of cream of wheat cooked in skim milk and brown sugar, changed into white cotton shorts and shirt and went to bed. Seven minutes after six. He set the clock-radio for nine o'clock. Three hours sleep before he got to school in time for his first class. Creative writing. Today's assignment: best first lines in fiction.

He fell asleep in less than five minutes; dreamed that his walls had sprouted roses of every color including black and green and he was standing at his front door ushering the neighbors in to see, when the voice on the radio woke him. "Bit of a problem on I-20 at Glenwood, doesn't look serious. Everything flowing on the downtown connector. Will talk to you in just a…"

They were waiting for him. Every seat taken. The women at the front, the men at the back. The women smiling, the men nonchalant or very solemn.

"Had a late night, Dr. Dirk? You look tired."

"Couldn't sleep. Indigestion," he said.

"Need a girlfriend, Dr. Dirk?"

"She probably gave him indigestion," a voice said from the back.

Hisses from the front.

"Okay, ladies and gentlemen. We have work to do."

"Do you have a girlfriend, Dr. Dirk?"

"Thanks for your concern, Ms. Vance, but we really do need to discuss more important things. Much more important things."

Hisses from the back.

"Let's begin now. Ms. Vance, what treasures did you find?"

"Ooh, I got some good ones, Dr. Dirk." Millie Vance stood, adjusted every piece of her clothing, smiled at Morton Dirk, cleared her throat. "First, from *Moby Dick* by Herman Melville: 'Call me Ishmael.'"

"Excellent, Ms. Vance," Dirk said, "and why is that simple, three-word sentence so powerful?"

"I don't know…it's just so mysterious…as if he's hiding something and doesn't want us to know who he really is and…"

"Go on please."

"And…it's the sound. You have to say it aloud." Her voice deepened: "'Call me Ishmael.' It's just good. Oh, and another one, from…"

Morton interrupted: "Very good, Ms. Vance, very good. But let us hear from someone else. Mr. Duc?"

"'124 was…'" Duc began.

"Toni Morrison," one of the women shouted.

"Thank you so much," Tran Duc said with exaggerated dignity. "So grateful."

"'It-was-the-best-of-times-it-was-the-worst-of-times-Charles-Dickens-*A-Tale-of-Two-Cities*,'" a man said quickly.

"Very good, Mr. Stanton, although it does go on a bit more, but that's the part that everyone remembers. Very good."

"Prof?" Millie Vance raised her hand.

"Ms. Vance?" Dirk asked.

"Another Toni Morrison, sir: 'Sth…' from *Jazz*," she said.

"Excellent, excellent, Ms. Vance. But that first word, what do you think it means. Anyone?"

"That's how black people say, 'T-s-k,' Professor Dirk," Millie said with finality.

"And who am I to argue with you, Ms. Vance," Morton Dirk said. "Let's go on." He nodded at a woman who had begun raising her hand—hesitantly.

"'In the beginning was the word, and the word was…'"

"Not the first line; and not usually considered fiction; Miss Franklyn. Remember?" Morton interrupted quickly.

"Yeah," several voices said.

"Anything else, Miss Franklyn?"

"'Many years later…, she began slowly, the sonority of her voice bearing the insistent weight of every word. Her eyes were on his face, but she was speaking to a distance.

Dirk felt his chest tighten and the skin of his face burn, before a wash of cold swept down to his feet. He had known that she would be the one to discover that first line; because she would look where he would.

Gaynor Franklyn continued. She could hear a voice prompting her, reading the lines for her. Another line, then a paragraph, and another. Unafraid, because the voice was strong and sure of itself, never giving her the freedom of altering what it said—demanding that she repeat every word and nuance.

The night before, she had read several pages, but had not committed anything to memory except the first sentence. She continued to speak, wondered where the voice came from. Another paragraph, and another, until she had recited two pages. Her knees began to weaken, and a hot-and-cold sensation climbed her legs until it stopped where her thighs met. Small pulses coursed through her pelvis. The words continued—even through her orgasm. When her contractions stopped, the voice slowed, then faded into the noise of her breathing. She stopped, exhausted, shivering.

"Garcia Marquez," Dirk finished for her. He held the Gaynor Franklyn's eyes until the latter fidgeted and turned away. Morton's gaze flickered, and suddenly he was looking at them, as if searching for their thoughts. The students looked at each other, shifted uncomfortably, avoided each other's eyes.

"I'm sorry, ladies and gentlemen, for allowing Ms. Franklyn to go on for so long, but while I lay awake last night, I kept saying that line to myself, wishing…with little hope that one of you would find that most precious gem. Few people want to tackle Garcia's *One Hundred Years of Solitude*. Thank you very much, Miss Franklyn…for this gift."

Gaynor Franklyn stared hard at him, frowning slightly, wanting to find the right question to ask him: Did you do that to me? But she could not force the thought into words.

After twenty minutes of presentations, Dirk raised both hands to silence the class. "Now, tell me, why do you think I asked you to do this assignment?"

"I know one thing, I'll never be a writer," a thin, serious man with thick, black rimmed glasses said.

"Go on, Mr. Russell."

"I'll never be able to come up with stuff like that. You know…."

"I don't know. But here is the point: good writing is not the result of typing three hundred pages of dialog and narration. Good writing is reading and love of reading. I know most of you took this class because you thought I could make you writers. No can do. I can share good writing with you, but I cannot teach you to write.

Do you know why I do not have too many contemporary writers in my courses—and why those few are mostly Nobel laureates? It is because I want you to read to learn. On your own, you can read for entertainment; that does not require much effort. But my recommended reading list is full of books that make you work. Many of them are boring, I know. Faulkner is not my favorite writer, but I made myself read everything he wrote. I do not enjoy reading books where black people are dismissed as "niggers," but I must discipline myself to get beyond that and pick out other things that are to my benefit. I want you to read to find things that you can imitate or even steal from other writers. Mind you, I do not want you plagiarizing the classics. That's transparent and cheap. But steal their imaginations. See how they used words, how they described people and events. How they structured their stories. Remember there was no bestseller list when Dickens wrote, but his books changed British society. My class is for teaching you to love language;

how to use words and grammar. Yes, grammar. Know the rules, so that when you break them, you do it deliberately, not from ignorance. This class is to teach you language, not how to write.

"That is the only way you can master the most powerful skill that the human mind has developed. Consider humanity's most marvelous achievements in art and science and architecture and literature. How could they have been conceived and effected by that misshapen ball of fat and nerves in our heads if not for language? Language is how one persuades another to give birth, to live, to do things...and to die."

Two students shivered. There was something in Dr. Dirks's voice that went beyond pleasantness: a persuasiveness as frightening as a sharp knife held against the throat. But no one ever mentioned it.

Morton Dirk continued, "For our next class, I want you to write down five topics of fiction: love, crime, mystery, horror, adventure. Give a title, subject, and a first line or paragraph that astounds you, and will make your classmates jealous."

"Dr. Dirk? How come you're not a writer? With all the stuff that you know, you'd think that you'd be a famous writer."

"Then I wouldn't have time to make all of you writers."

A few students smiled uncertainly; they had seen his hesitation before he answered. He couldn't tell them that he did write: short stories on pornographic crime; using the newspaper reports of his hits. He had sold every story under a pseudonym. If anyone was able to make the connection to him, he would be happy to show the clippings.

None of his students missed Morton Dirk's classes unless for a very good reason; and those who did, begged to see the notes of a classmate. Dr. Dirk's classes set them free of the small spaces circumscribed by desks and chairs; set them on voyages down the Americas, across Europe, into Africa, around Asia, and through the Pacific.

In the fifty minutes they spent with him, they were pulled into a maelstrom of elation, horror, laughter, mystery, and terror. When he recited passages from their reading assignments, they heard the voices of the authors and characters; saw them again in their dreams and nightmares. But always, it was their own voices recalling passages read by Dirk. Never his voice. And his face disappeared as soon as they walked out of his class.

A watch chimed. Faces lifted to the clock above the classroom door. They waited for a last word. Professor Morton Dirk rubbed his palms together as if acceding to the forced completion of the day. They pushed back from the desks. Stood up slowly as if apologetic for the interruption of his thoughts.

As soon as the voices of the students has disappeared down the hall, Dirk forced himself to pick up his papers and books and to head to the parking lot with deliberate slowness. Going home. No big hurry to go anyplace special.

After his telephone call from the airport, Morton stopped at a strip-mall parking lot where a sign offered car washing and detailing. "Don't forget to remove the floor mats and vacuum the carpet…and the seats. Please."

"Yes, sir."

He gave a three-dollar tip.

"Ain't a germ left in this car, sir," the cleaner said.

"I know, that's why I come here."

"Thank you, sir. Come again."

"Yes," he said, but he would not return to that cleaner for several months—before his face became recognizable and familiar; and the questions began: What was his name? What did he do? Where did he live? He did not want any of it. No familiarity, no brotherhood.

He toyed with the idea of someday answering truthfully the questions about his profession: "I kill people. I'm very good at it; and I'm well paid for it." He could imagine the initial shocked expression, then laughter, then the relief of appreciation: "You're so funny…for a couple of seconds I believed you.…You were so serious when you said that. Almost believed you, you know." The head would shake in mock reproach, "Careful, somebody might take you seriously.…"

His victims resisted believing too. Refused to accept the imminence of their deaths. Searched, even as their eyes closed, to find some way of escaping his knife; of stopping the blood rushing out of their throats; of plugging the bullet hole; of waking from the nightmare; of finding the right words to change his mind, or for promising the right price for their lives.

He wondered what his students would do with their memories of him if they ever discovered the truth about their teacher. Would they discard what they had learned from him, because he had tainted the truth. Then again, what the hell? He had his life to live. Had to make himself die for a moment after every kill, to forget the victims' faces and their voices. He did not enjoy killing any more than a surgeon enjoyed slicing through a patient's skin and muscle. Each killing was an obligation to his father's organization…and he was well compensated for his skills. He had to put recollections into their compartments. Like the parents of Tran Duc: smothering their memories of Saigon: disemboweled bodies; limbs detached by the sudden orange thundering wrench of mines, and sent flying through the air to land at one's feet; cheeks clawed open by fragments of stone and concrete from bullets and shrapnel splattering against walls; ground and air shaking from bombs screaming from the sky. The nightmares that had been soothed by the touch of American percale sheets, the comfort of conditioned air, a fifteen-hundred-dollar used car that needed only two hundred and eighty-seven dollars in repairs, and an apartment balcony filled with potted annuals—mostly yellows and whites. Bad memories were put into compartments, and hidden under bargains at discount malls.

That night, Tran tried to tell his parents what he had experienced in Dr. Dirk's class. Made their eyes shine with his infectious excitement, and they forgot to remind him that he should concentrate on science.

"What does he look like, this Mr. Duck?" Mrs. Duc asked in Vietnamese.

Tran paused for a long time, as if surprised at the question. He could not recall Morton Dirk's face. "He's black, a little tall, slim. But I can't remember what he looks like or whom he looks like."

"He's ugly or handsome?" Mr. Duc asked.

Tran shrugged. "Don't know. The women in the class all fall in love with him when they come into the room, but nobody talks about him that way outside. It's as if he leaves your mind when you're not looking at him."

"He must be a very good teacher, if what you remember is what he says, and not what he looks like," Tran's father said.

Mrs. Duc agreed. "Very good teacher." The thought of Professor Dirk was a good one to hold on to, good to cover the bad memories. They hoped he had a happy family–with at least two children.

Saturday morning: vacuum, wash, dust. Saturday afternoon: two hours working out at the YMCA. Afterwards, he had to cook chili for the men's shelter. He went to a pay telephone at a nearby supermarket. "Jude? It's Morton. How you doing?"

"Don't think I'm gonna walk out of the hospital this time, man. You coming by? When?…Okay. Lemme see, I don't know…they won't let me eat anything useful in this damn' hospital. Bring a bunch of grapes…hide a chocolate with raisins in the bag. Shit. I'm gonna die soon. I don't see why I can't have some ribs and stuff."

"I'll see you later, Jude. If you look like you're going to die, I'll take you out of there and we can go to a rib place. You can eat until you burst."

"Yeah, let's do that tonight."

"See you."

He went to the supermarket cafeteria and sat at a corner table in the rear to drink a lemonade. If Jude suffered much longer, he would have to end his friend's life. He could not endure another's pain.

He went back to the produce section for the ingredients for beef chili. Five pounds of ground chuck, onions, chives, cilantro, red, green and yellow bell peppers, tomatoes, a jar of chili powder. He had enough garlic at home.

At the register, the cashier's fingers brushed his palm as she handed him change. She did not bother lifting her eyes to his face: hands too hard—probably a construction worker. She focused on moving the chewing gum to the other side of her mouth. He paused, thought of telling her that she was pretty. She looked up, her head tilted slightly, waiting for another stupid flirtation. Already bored. Saw his cold flat eyes. Frowned, and kept her eyes on the bag as she handed it to him. Forgot to remind him to have a nice day, and to come again.

Two hours later, at home, he turned off the burner under the pot of chili; then showered to get the smell of cooking off himself, and put the stock pot into a cardboard box. He put that on the floor on the passenger side of his car and drove downtown to the men's shelter.

The superintendent was opening pots to smell their contents. He reminded Morton of the soft-hearted Sergeant Schultz on the old television show *Hogan's Heroes*. Perhaps the superintendent had fought on Hitler's behalf. No, too young. But what better place to hide and forget than in a men's shelter in Atlanta? Morton was sure the superintendent was hiding from something, or had escaped from somewhere. Inconceivable that one could be so altruistic as to dedicate his life to caring for the city's human discards. His name was Berger. Could be German. Could be a saint. Could be a hired assassin…or a police informant.

"Talk to Jude lately?" the superintendent asked him.

"Yes, earlier today. Going to see him later. Didn't sound too good. Wish I could take him some chili."

"Think he'll make it?"

"No, Jude's not coming back here."

"Son of a bitch was such a pain when he came here first time, wanted to tell us how to run the place, and he couldn't run his own life. It was you brought him here?"

"Yeah. He came into my class one morning. Said he wanted to write his life story, and somebody had told him to attend one of my classes. Dirty, fetid, and dread-locked. The students walked out, and security put him out and called the police. I gave him my number at school and asked him to call me later. Called the next day and asked me to meet him in Piedmont Park, near the lake. Picked him up there and eventually persuaded him to let me bring him here. It was the only place where I could remember seeing lines of homeless men."

"That guy loved you. Used to tell the other guys you were several types of genius. Knew everything about anything. Used to try and speak like you too. Poor Jude. Had everything ending in 'itis', plus diabetes and cirrhosis. So, did you help him write his life story?"

"No, when he started talking about it, he realized that his life wasn't different from most of the men he hung out with; and I guess he didn't want to remind himself that he had messed up."

"I'll miss him," Dirk said. "I wish I had asked him more about himself."

"What did you guys get to talk about?"

"Me? Not much. Jude did all the talking…about the people he had met; places he'd been. Not a word about himself or his family. Know anything about them?"

"We have a little file on each of our long-term customers. But I don't think his wife's name and address is in there. Don't know if he had children."

Morton Dirk went to Piedmont Hospital at six in the evening. Could not understand how the shrunken brown body on the bed had found the strength to use the telephone; and to have spoken for so long. So much worse in the week since his last visit.

Morton could not bring himself to ask how his friend was. "Brought you the grapes…and the chocolate. Thought of bringing some chicken, but they'd smell it."

Jude's face wrinkled. "You could'a told them it was for yourself."

"Then they'd come in here and find you sucking on a bone."

"Anyway, you'd better bring the chicken soon...and some ribs. No corn, I couldn't..." Jude stopped, exhausted.

Dirk watched Jude's chest struggle to suck in a little more air. "Take it easy," he said. "You want me to raise your head a bit?"

Jude nodded. "Know something? I'm really afraid of dying. I don't know what I'd want to live for...but I'm scared, man...really scared. This dying business don't make no sense at all. Why we gotta die, man?"

"You're getting too deep for me, Jude. I can't answer these questions."

"I'm too young for this, man. I know I look like ancient crap, but I'm only forty-one...young enough to be your damn' brother. How about you?"

"Thirty-two."

"You got kids?"

"No. You?"

"Nah. That's not right. A man shouldn't die without kids. If you got a kid, you don't really die, you know. Kid's half of you...so half of you goes on living, until...until the kid's got another kid...then quarter of you goes on living again. After that, I guess it don't matter. You should have a kid...two kids."

"That would be two halves, Jude. And if I had four kids that would be two of me."

Jude's body shook, and he winced with the pain that his weak laughter caused. "Man, you're smart. I didn't think of that. You should marry a woman like my wife...smart like you. Really, really smart...teaches science in college. Good-looking woman, too." He shook his head and stared at the ceiling. "I was jealous of my wife. Used to get me pissed when she..."

"She what?"

"Nothing." Jude turned his hands, palms upwards. "Used to do good things with these hands.... Listen, Prof, if I don't make it out of here, go see my wife, man. Tell her something good about me. Can't think of anything, but you can come up with some good shit. And I just changed my mind about dying…I want to frigging die.…Now. You want to turn up the volume on the TV? Remote on the table by the lamp."

Dirk turned his chair to face the television. During a news break, there was a story about a body identified as that of a prominent Savannah attorney found on a beach near Keller, south of the city. The victim's throat had been slashed with a very sharp instrument. The victim's wallet contained one hundred and thirteen dollars, so robbery may not have been the motive. The Police had no immediate leads.

Neither of the two men paid much attention. Same thing every day on the news. A nurse came in to bring a tray with Jude's supper. "Smell that shit. Enough to make a man puke. I'm beginning to hate food. Why don't they just bring me a case of beer and let me die drunk…and happy?"

"Yes, everybody says the same thing about hospital food. Try and eat something, anyway."

"Too late, man. I just want to sleep."

"You want me to read you something?"

"Guess I'd better start reading the bible…just in case. Look in the drawer, bound to be one in there."

Dirk took out the mottled green and black Gideon bible, rested its spine on his knee, opened it down the middle with his thumbs. He scanned the left page quickly: JOB 36, 37. His eyes stopped at the last verses at the bottom of the page. He began to read:

"At this my heart trembleth, and is moved out of this place. Hear attentively the noise of his voice, and the sound that goeth out of his mouth.

He directeth it under the whole heaven, and his lightning unto the ends of the earth.

After it a voice roareth: he thundereth with the voice of his excellency; and he will not stay them when his voice is heard."

The words wrapped themselves about Jude Delaware, warmed him and lifted his body until he could not feel the ridges and folds of the sheet and mattress. The pain in his chest flowed out with each breath, and when he closed his eyes he continued to see a cloudless blue sky. He lay very still, afraid to disturb the illusion. Then he began to fall. He panicked at first, wanted to call out to Jude to grab hold of his hand. But it was impossible to move anything. He was shooting downwards now, and winced at the thought of his body slamming into the floor of the hospital basement. Perhaps he should tell Morton how it felt to die. He was certain that Morton's voice was somehow related to his dying. He opened his mouth slightly to ask; and to say that he wasn't angry. And the air sighed out of his lungs.

Morton waited for five minutes after Jude's chest had stopped moving, then went to the nurses' station. "Could you check on my friend in room four eleven. I think he's stopped breathing."

The nurse picked up the telephone, dialed four digits, spoke briefly, and hurried into Jude's room; then a doctor walked past quickly and entered the room. A few minutes later, the doctor came out and walked over to him. "You're Mr. Delaware's friend?"

"Yes."

"I'm afraid he's just passed away. He seems to have died peacefully."

"Thank you. I'll make arrangements for his funeral. And I'll inform his relatives. Thanks."

"I'm very sorry."

Dirk called the superintendent at the shelter from the hospital lobby. "Can you try and locate his wife? I'll make arrangements with a funeral home. For cremation, if we can't find her in a couple of days. Can't afford to wait too long. Know where Jude came from?"

"Denver, I think. I'll call the Salvation Army there. We get these situations. Should get some info before the week's out."

"You're a big help, man. Thanks."

"Okay. Thanks, Professor Dirk, Jude was lucky having a friend like you."

"Talk with you later."

He stopped at a grocery for a copy of the Atlanta Constitution; checked to see that it carried the story of the attorney's death. It was on page A9 with a photograph of the man smiling.

At eight that evening, he drove to a strip mall two miles away from his home. Went to a pay telephone outside a drugstore.

"It's Morton. Need anything?"

"Sure. Where?"

"The yellow one?"

"No, I prefer the blue. Smells newer. What time?"

"Ten."

"Bring a story. I'll be ready in…about an hour."

"Okay. Bye."

Dirk showered and changed into gray wool slacks, light-blue shirt with a red and blue rep tie, black cotton socks, cordovan tasseled Bass loafers, and a navy blazer. He put a small radio with a compact disc player into a black leather carry-on suitcase, and a compact disc of Ravel's Bolero. He wedged in a leather toiletry case, and slipped a manuscript into the zippered outside pocket.

He left his home at nine, and drove to a motel painted light blue with white trim. He asked for a room at the back on the ground floor. "Really tired. Want to be away from the noise of the traffic…and the bright lights."

"There you go, sir. Room one-oh-six. Call us if there's any problem."

"Thank you very much. Appreciate it."

He examined the room carefully, checked the bed linens, opened all the drawers of the dresser, looked under the bed. Then he went to the telephone. "Blue, room one-oh-six. What time?"

"About forty-five minutes. Brought a good story?"

"The best."

"See you."

He removed his jacket, tie and shoes, turned off the lights and turned the radio on. He went to sit in an armchair near the door, and placed his feet on the bed. He did not move until he heard the soft tap on the door. He turned the radio off. The red figures on the radio's clock read ten twelve. It would be worth the money...as usual.

She came in quickly. Removed a floppy, black beret and large tortoiseshell glasses. She unbuttoned her oversized denim shirt, kicked off her tennis shoes, and stepped out of her baggy jeans.

She was dressed in a black body stocking. No ornamentation, not even a watch. "How much you think that's worth?" she asked.

He turned on a bedside lamp. Looked long at her body, asked her to turn around. "At least five hundred," he said. He took the manuscript from the suitcase, and threw it on the bed. Removed the radio from the case, plugged the cord into a wall receptacle and inserted the disc, but did not turn it on. He undressed and went to sit naked on the bed with his legs spread apart.

She peeled the suit off slowly, smiling at the effect on him, watching as his breathing grew faster. He never took his eyes off her. "Your body must be the most glorious piece of art I will ever see." he said.

She turned around slowly. "Like?"

He nodded.

She climbed on the bed and sat between his legs. "Nice. So, anything interesting happened to you today?"

"No, nothing. You?"

"Nada...except for right now," she answered.

He reached for the manuscript.

"How many pages?" she asked.

"Eighteen," he said.

She wriggled against him. "Good."

He started reading slowly. By the fifth page, she was breathing as heavily as if she had just ended a hard race. At the last page, she was covered with a fine sheen of sweat, and both hands were between her legs. She moaned and rubbed her back against his chest. He turned the disc player on, and turned off the lights. She let him stretch out on the bed then threw herself down on him as if he were the first meal she had eaten in days. They did not stop until the end of *Bolero*.

She rolled off him when her breathing had settled, and went into the bathroom to shower. He went in after her, then came to lie on the bed with her again.

"Good?" she asked.

He smiled. She closed her eyes and after a few minutes, he could hear her snoring softly. He moved carefully so that he did not wake her. Half an hour later, she opened her eyes, yawned and stretched out her arms. "Read to me again." And an hour and a half later, she lay on her stomach and spread her arms and legs so that each limb was pointed to a corner of the bed. "You don't have to read, this time," she said.

At four in the morning, she started dressing. When she was done, he took an unsealed envelope from the inside pocket of his jacket, and handed it to her. She opened it. "Ooh, five new Franklins."

"Tuition," he said.

She returned his grin. "See you in class, Monday, Prof." And left.

But this time a small loneliness remained: made him think of Jude's wife. Smart and good-looking, Jude had said. Some day, it would be good to have a regular woman–not a wife, just somebody regular whom he didn't have to pay for intimacy. Somebody to cook for. He frowned. Angry at the sentimentality he was beginning to enjoy. But it would be good to see Jude's wife. In a way, she now belonged to him.

He was home at six thirty. Sunday morning: catch up on sleep before another two-hour work out at the Y. He spent the afternoon reading his students' assignments. Made himself a supper of grilled salmon, baked potato, and a tomato and lettuce salad. At ten o'clock precisely, his telephone rang. He waited. After three rings it stopped. Thirty seconds later, it rang again. He picked it up at the forth ring. Waited.

"See you did a good job. As expected. Checked your money yet?"

"Yes, it's there."

"Got a trip for you in two weeks. Sunday, the twenty-eighth. Houston."

"Yes."

The caller waited. They listened to each other's breathing.

"Yes…Dad," Morton Dirk said.

There was a click, then the dial tone.

He put the handset down. His mouth tight with anger. "Son of a bitch…son of a bitch…son of a bitch," he said to the telephone—very softly, suspicious that the machine was listening.

He was not anybody's son. He was not even certain that she was human: too cold, too efficient, too contemptuous of ordinary vulnerabilities. He was not comfortable with the new emotions that were beginning to stir about somewhere at the edge of his memories. It was as if some memories had awakened after sixteen years, and were stiff from their long inactivity; like the grub-like aliens of science fiction that lie dormant in their human hosts until the required stimulus musters them.

He squeezed his eyes and shook his head, the vague sounds and feelings disappeared. He ran through all the things to do the next day–no errors, no omissions, no hesitations. He had to remain busy and invisible: caring for the poor and homeless, working his flower beds, nurturing his students. A credit to his race and community. Like the sainted Augustus Telamon. Another time, when he was calmer, he would return to the thought of killing his "dad."

3

Sixteen years ago: Sunday, two days after his graduation from high school, and five hours after returning home from celebrating his graduation, Morton Dirk's parents died.

At four in the morning, two men entered his parents' bedroom. There had not been any sound of entrance; no sound of footsteps on the stairs or in the hallway outside Morton's bedroom. No sound—until his door opened, and a figure filling the doorway said, "Your parents want you in their room. Now." An automatic pistol with a silencer hung from his left hand.

Morton screamed, "Dad!"

"Shut...up," the man said. He lifted the gun slightly.

Morton clenched his teeth, and walked quickly to his parents' room; the gunman behind him.

His parents were on their knees at their bedside with their clasped hands stretched out on the tossed blanket as if in prayer to the other man sitting at the other side of the bed. The floor around his parent's knees was dark with urine. Morton tried to shout for help, but his throat had frozen. When he tried to move toward his parents, his knees buckled, and he fell to the floor. The sitting man turned to look at him.

A light brown face with no expression of concern or interest. Wearing a dark brown suit with an open-necked black shirt, and black shoes. His face vague as if a private fog persisted around him. No movement, even of breathing.

Then the sitting man turned to his parents. "Mr. and Mrs. Dirk. Do you have here, in this house, the money you stole from Caraglo?"

The father shook his head.

The man continued, "Are you able to pay us, without accrued interest, the hundred and sixty-five thousand seven hundred dollars you stole?"

Both parents shook their heads.

"How much money do you have available at this moment, in this house?"

"Two...two hundred and something dollars," the father said.

The man turned to the woman. "How much?"

"Two hundred and thirty," she said.

"How much does your son have?"

They looked at him.

It took him about half a minute to force the words out. "About twelve dollars...in my wallet."

"Two hundred and forty-two dollars, cash." The man said, his voice serene and unhurried, as if he were reading them a bedside story. "Tonight, Mr. and Mrs. Dirk, you are going to die. You will both be shot in the head at close range to ensure a quick, painless, and certain death. I cannot offer you my condolences, as I have no choice or regrets in this matter. I was sent to collect the money you owed, or to kill you if you did not have it. You do not have it. Therefore, I must kill you. We cannot change anything about your circumstances at this point. Please place your heads down on the mattress."

He looked at the other man standing behind the kneeling couple. Nodded.

The other man moved back one step, stretched out his arm and put the tip of the silencer near the back of the woman's head, and the mattress was suddenly red with pink and yellow clots and fragments of brain and bone. Before his father could speak or move, his head had exploded in another shower of gray, yellow, and white. The only noise had been the dull, sudden percussion from the gun, like two muted coughs.

The assassin turned toward Morton, the gun already steady and aimed at his head; a small white cloud rising from the barrel as if from a cigarette. He looked at his partner. At that moment, Morton felt a sudden coldness sweep his body, as if he were waiting for the insertion of a hypodermic needle. He looked more closely at the killer: pale white skin, balding although he appeared to be only thirty, gray eyes, gray baggy suit, a white shirt buttoned at the collar, and black shoes. And a faint upward curve in the line of his lips, as if proud of his efficiency.

The sitting man shook his head and rose. "No, let's go." He rose and walked out of the door. The gunman followed, closing the door gently after himself. Neither had even glanced at Morton as they left.

For two hours, Morton Dirk sat in his urine and feces. Oblivious to the wetness and stench in the room. His mother's body lay slumped on the bed. His father's body had jerked back and was lying on its back with the mouth grinning at the ceiling. The upper part of the face was a wet mass of shredded tissue.

Morton tried to stand, but found the effort too difficult. Squatted for a few minutes then stood up slowly, and walked to the telephone on the bedside table. He touched the handset, and pulled his hand back quickly to stop the acid vomit that rushed into his mouth. Turned around and bent forward, clutching his stomach. Retched until he could bring up nothing but droplets of saliva. He wiped his hand on the carpet and picked up the telephone. There was no dial tone. He leaned against the table with both hands and breathed deeply. Until his trembling stopped, and he felt his heartbeats quiet, and his breathing slow. His hands and feet grew cold; as if he were out in the snow without gloves and shoes. He put his hands against his cheeks; they were painfully cold to the touch. He panicked and turned to the mirror; relaxed slightly—he wasn't dead.

He was breathing normally again. He looked around the room, and walked over to the bodies. Touched his mother's shoulder, and went and stood over his father's body. No revulsion at the face with its head torn away over the eyes. No more terror.

There were things to do: call the police; call his parent's attorney and his mother's sister—his only known relative—in Chicago; find a place to stay. He would probably spend the night in a police cell—the first person the police would suspect. He went downstairs, certain the men had left. The front and back doors were locked, no broken windows, no sign of the men's entry.

He went back upstairs and removed his soiled shorts. Pulled on a pair of sweat pants, went outside and rang a neighbor's doorbell. A woman looked through the curtains in a side window. She opened the door. "Hello Morton…" then she saw the vomit on his tee-shirt.

"Call the police please. My parents…"

She screamed and rushed back into the house. Her husband came to the door. "Holy shit." And he went back in to call the police.

Morton heard their hushed voices, and they came back to the door. "What's happened to your parents, Morton?"

"Two men came in during the night. Killed them."

The woman began making moaning sounds. The man began to tremble. Morton turned back to his house. Heard the door close behind him and the thud of the double-bolt lock.

He left his front door unlocked, and sat on the bottom stair to wait. Five minutes later, three police cars came, and four policemen with shotguns and drawn pistols came to the door. He opened the door for them. "My parents' bodies are upstairs. I'm the only other person here."

The police searched every room and closet. They cordoned off the street; asked neighbors if they had heard anything unusual during the night; searched the grounds around the house; whispered among themselves; asked him the same questions a hundred times. Other men in plain clothes came and took photographs and specimens. Measured everything. Morton sat on the stairs.

He relaxed. It would be interesting sleeping in a police station. The police told him to pack enough clothes for a week. They made him put a windbreaker over his head when he left the house. He could hear the "zzzip" of camera drives and the lightning of their flashes on the ground. Wondered how they could have got to his home so quickly.

They took him to the police station, and allowed him to call his parent's attorney. Brian Holler sounded as if he had heard Morton confess to the murders; then struggled to regain his composure. He began by telling Morton that everything would be all right. "Yes," Morton said.

More questions: No, he did not hear the men come in. Did not hear shots. Awakened by the sound of a car's engine starting. Did not look out; went to the bathroom. Saw his parent's bedroom door open, and the light on, but no sound; peeped in and saw the bodies. He had gone to the bathroom to wipe himself and to change his pants, and to call the police. Asked the neighbors to call the police. Took the police into his parents' room. Tried not to look at the bodies again. Showed where he had soiled himself and sat for two hours in the stinking mess. That was all.

He gave the police the name and address of the import-export business where his parents had worked, but did not tell them that his parents were incompetent crooks who had stolen from the company. Let them find that out for themselves. There were some things he had decided: he would not leave Atlanta; he would kill the man who had shot his parents. He was surprised at his feelings about the other man—as much admiration as hate. But he would find him too. If his parents' past employers managed to evade the law, he would destroy every piece of their property, then kill them.

He was put in a cell smelling of pine disinfectant. In the dim light, he looked for faces in the patterns left by the peeling paint on the wall at the foot of the bed. He fell asleep thinking of Italian sports cars.

At nine o'clock the next night, the police secreted him into an unmarked car with darkened windows. "We're taking you to a safe house," the officer sitting next to him said.

"Where?" Morton asked.

"We're not supposed to tell you. You may tell someone by accident…on the 'phone."

They said nothing more until the car pulled into the driveway of a ranch-style yellow-brick house. The garage door was already rising as they turned off the street. A door opened and Morton could see into a kitchen. A black couple was waiting. The man was bald, built like a power lifter, and had a deeply cleft chin. The woman was slightly plump with eyes like obsidian marbles; had a square face with a delicate pointed chin that did not seem to belong to the face; and a wide comforting mouth. She smiled at Morton, but her eyes did not. Then she looked at the driver. "Nobody behind you," she said.

The man stretched out his hand to Morton. "I'm Leonard Sight. My partner is Destine Hills. We're going to look after you…until you can move to somewhere safer. So, if anybody aks, you're our nephew who just moved to Atlanta from West Virginia to check out some Atlanta colleges. The neighbors know us as Mr. and Mrs. Spight. We're supposed to be business reps…so we're hardly ever home."

"You'll be all right with us, hon," Destine Hills said. We've always taken good care of our guests. And don't worry about my sexy self. I'm one bad policewoman." She extended her hand.

"Yeah," Spight said, "she makes a lot of money arm wrestling guys…and winning."

"And she can drink too," the driver of the car said.

"Time to get your stupid ass out of here, DeMarco," she said. "All of you. We got to get this gentleman comfortable."

"See you all." The men who had brought Morton went into the garage. "You'll be all right," one said to Morton.

They heard the garage door close. Spight locked the kitchen door. He knew the jokes had been for everyone's benefit: to hide their discomfort with him; and to ease his discomfort with them. He could see the mixture of pity and relief in their eyes—relief that it was not their parents or relatives who had been killed. They would be polite, make conversation, but keep their distance. He was already contaminated by kinship to "those people" who found trouble and easy money irresistible.

Destine Hills took a baked ham from the oven. "I'll make you a sandwich, hon. What do you want on it? We've got lettuce, tomato, mayo, mustard. Everything?"

The boy nodded. He knew the "hon" was automatic—but he liked it.

"Don't eat too much tonight. Drink a glass of hot milk...it'll make you sleep. I'll make you a serious breakfast tomorrow," she said.

The telephone rang at midnight exactly. Spight picked it up after the first ring. "Morton Dirk is in no danger," the voice said. Our dispute was with his parents. The matter is settled."

They let him sleep until eight o'clock the next morning. "Poor kid," Destine Hills said, "don't think he got a minute of sleep last night."

"Guess we're gonna have to move out of here soon," Spight said, "I didn't sleep myself. Wonder how these bastards knew where the boy was. And they've got the number to this place, too. You know something?" he continued, "that voice scared me shitless...but I think the guy was serious. I suspect nobody's gonna come after the kid. What's the point? He didn't see anything...or hear anything."

"What did the caller sound like?" Destine asked.

"Piece of ice."

"I'm glad the station's got a couple of cars down the road, although..." she did not finish.

Spight nodded. He moved toward the doorway. "Eight o'clock, I'm going to see if he's up," he said, and went into the hallway. He tapped softly on the bedroom door.

"I'm up," Morton said.

"Help yourself, hon...and if you need anything else, just ask," Destine said to Morton, when he came into the kitchen. "So, how'd you sleep?"

"Now and then. 'Phone made me jump."

"Headquarters just checking," Morley said.

While they were eating, the telephone rang again. Spight answered it. He spoke to Morton when he came back to the table. "Looks like we'll be here for the rest of the week. Judge August Telamon wants to talk to you, Mr. Dirk. Major said he'd be here tomorrow evening. They'll call and let us know the time tomorrow. And your lawyer, Mr. Martin Holler, is going to call you later."

"Telamon...the Supreme Court judge?" Morton asked.

"Same...man who runs Atlanta," Delaware said.

"And a lot of Georgia," Spight said.

"What the hell's he doing with Morton?" Destine asked.

Delaware shrugged. "Sure would like to be in with the judge...I can tell you that."

August Telamon arrived at nine-thirty that night. He brought a new quiet into the house.

"Evening, Judge."

"Good evening, Judge."

"Judge Telamon."

"Good evening, all." Judge Telamon warmed them individually with his smile. "Ah, there's Mr. Dirk. Mr. Dirk, I am really, very, very sorry about your family. This is a situation beyond anyone's capacity to bear alone. It was too much for me...and I tell you, I have known some in my career." He looked at Spight. "Is there some place where Mr. Dirk and I can speak?"

"Yes, Judge." And Leonard Spight led them into a small conference room. Closed the door, and left.

As soon as they were seated, Judge Telamon leaned toward Morton. "The police contacted your aunt in Chicago. Told her what happened.

She's terrified of you moving in with her. Afraid that the killers will follow you to her home. Put the 'phone down on the officer who called her."

Morton nodded. "I can understand."

"How do you feel about your situation. We don't want to keep you here…really imprisoned indefinitely. Is there any other relative we can contact? Anywhere?"

"No, my parents didn't keep in touch with anybody…any family. Just the people they worked with. And I'm not sure about these people."

Judge Telamon rose and walked the periphery of the room. Sighed, and returned to his seat. "I have a suggestion. You can try it for a couple of weeks, and…then decide. It will be up to you. We will do all we can to help, because I find it impossible not to become personally involved in a situation this unspeakable. I do not have a family. My wife died in a car accident ten years ago. I live alone…but have a small house staff. I would be very happy if you came to stay with me until you found some place where you'd be comfortable."

Morton looked intently at Judge Telamon. "But you don't know me…."

"We are checking everything about your family. We have to. You're an A student. Always at the top of your class. Best in your class in mathematics and languages. Never been in trouble, very persuasive, very well spoken. You're an unusual young man, Mr. Dirk. Not too many have your discipline and talent."

"Yes," Morton Dirk said.

Judge Telamon's eyebrows rose. He did not understand what Morton had agreed to. "Yes?" he repeated.

"Yes, I'll take your offer. Thanks. I am very grateful."

Judge Telamon looked as if he were about to rise into the air like a black anthropomorphic balloon. "Good, good, good. You'll never regret this, Morton. I can promise you that. And don't worry about your safety at my home. Nobody's stupid enough to try anything there." He paused, tilted his head to the left as he waited for Morton's questions.

Morton stared directly at the judge, looking for signs of what was really running through the large round head. Impenetrable. He shook his head. "No, not right now…too much to think about…but I am very grateful."

"I believe that one day, I shall be the grateful one," Judge Telamon said.

The family attorney called at three in the afternoon. "How are you doing, Morton?"

"I'd like to get out, but they're taking care of me."

"I'm really sorry to have to bring these things up, but I have to take care of some family stuff. You think you can handle it now?"

"Yes, we'd better get it over with," Morton replied.

"Okay, if you think you can handle it. Your parents left instructions on what to do if anything happened to them. There's some insurance money to cover funeral expenses. They didn't have much coverage, and after the necessary things, there won't be much coming to you."

"How much," Morton asked.

"About seventeen thousand," Holler replied.

"I see. What funeral arrangements have you made?"

"Well, it's up to you. What do *you* want?"

"Cremation."

"Cremation?"

"Yes…and I don't think they'll let me attend the funeral. Let me know later where their remains are so I can visit the grave. I want them buried together."

Morton did not feel it necessary to explain to the attorney why he was not more distraught about the circumstances of his parents' deaths. From his first year in middle school, he had begun to distance himself emotionally from them when they showed little interest in his unusual intellect. They were dead, he wanted to remind Holler, leaving him with unanticipated and bothersome problems.

"All right, Mr. Dirk. I'll do as you wish. Again, my sincere condolences. Goodbye."

In his Peachtree Center office, Martin Holler put down the telephone slowly. Frowned. "That kid's cold, man. Cold," he said to himself. He put on his jacket. "I'm going down to the food-court for a coffee," he said to the secretary.

"There's coffee in the machine," she said.

"Yeah, but I want a lot of people around me," he said.

The following Saturday evening, Leonard Spight and Destine Hills drove Morton in an unmarked gray Ford Taurus, to Judge Telamon's home in North Buckhead. Six days after his parents' murder.

"I don't think anything will make up for your parents, Morton," Leonard said, "but Judge Telamon is good people. You're with the best. Take care of yourself, man."

"Look, if you still don't have a girlfriend in a month, give me a call. You can come over and learn to cook, and...."

"Destine. Let's go." Leonard pulled her away.

They shook hands with him, and turned toward to the car.

"Thank you very much, both of you. And the others too. Thanks," Morton Dirk said.

"Sure," Leonard Spight answered.

"Know something?" Destine asked when they were about half a mile away. "That kid handled his parents' death pretty cool. You think he was mixed up in it?"

"Nah, that was a professional hit, both people hit exactly in the same spot," Spight said. "Special hollow slugs, opened up as soon as they hit flesh. Kid couldn't handle stuff like that. Parents were crooks, too. Detectives suspect they stole from Caraglo."

"Shit. They worked for Caraglo? They should'a known they couldn't steal from him and get away. Stupid...really stupid."

"Yep, but Caraglo never put a hit on any body. Just breaks some bones."

"So, first time," Destine said. "They must've stolen a lotta cash."

"Stupid parents, but they had a bright kid."

"Sure is bright, but a little strange. Used to recite poetry all the time in the kitchen. Really nice stuff. Used to get me so hot sometimes, I wanted to drag his hard little butt in the bedroom."

"You crazy, woman?"

"Getting old and horny," Destine replied. They were silent until Spight stopped at a red light. "Another strange thing," Destine said, "I could never remember what he looked like when he went outa the room. You noticed?"

"You're right, now I couldn't tell you what he looked like, just that he was taller than me and sorta thin. And I always wanted him to speak...voice was relaxing," Spight said.

"Yeah. Relaxing. Like you were waiting for him to ask you to do something. But he never asked nobody anything. If I saw him on the street right now, don't think I'd recognize him. Anyway...so what you doing later? Destine asked.

"Going home. Ain't seen my old lady in a week," Spight said.

"Tomorrow won't make no difference. Come jump my bones tonight. Ain't had a man in...hell, can't even remember."

"I'll come quietly, Officer," Leonard said.

Earlier that day, Gabriel "Archangel" Caraglo, had sat in his attorney's office giving the same answers to the same questions. "Listen, Herm, I'm saying this for the last frigging time...you hear me? Just because I got a name that sound Italian, it don't mean I kill people that steal my money. You steal my money; you mess with me or my family; you interfere with my business, and I break your legs or your arms. I wreck your house or burn your car. But I don't kill people. I don't want that on my conscience. I believe in Hell, Herm. I'm a good Catholic. For the last time again, I didn't kill Dirk and his wife."

"Okay, okay. I believe you, Angel, but the police can't figure why somebody would call a hit on two folks for a hundred and sixty-five thousand dollars...money they stole from you."

"So how did the police know the prick and the bitch stole money from me," Caraglo asked.

"I don't know. They said somebody called them. Caller said his business was with the parents; that's why he left the kid alone," Herm Morille said.

"So, you telling me somebody found out that the Dirks were stealing money from me; knew how much they stole; and put a hit on the thieves for me. What kinda shit is that?"

"You see my problem, Angel?" I got to convince a judge that somebody did you a favor you didn't want."

"What else the police got on me?" Caraglo asked.

"That's it. You had a motive. You got a bad temper. You break people's legs. You wreck...."

"Enough already," Caraglo was screaming, "I know what I said." The sweat was running down his arms and sides. "Somebody wanted these folks dead...and set me up. What the hell I'm gonna do, Herm?"

"You look bad, Angel, go home and get some sleep. Tell Angelica we're gonna work this out. Kiss her and the children for me." Morille rose from his desk to let Gabriel Caraglo out.

"I can open the door for myself," Caraglo said. "Get me out of this shit, Herm. You hear?"

"I hear you, Angel," Morille said.

4

Before they begged him to be judge, August W. Telamon was the best lawyer in the South East and all the way west to El Paso, Texas. Made so much money, the Democrats and Republicans used to see his face when they spoke of God. That was all most people knew about Judge Telamon. Even those who had followed his career for four decades. Even those who worked closely with him.

Judge Telamon lived well. Five bedroom, cream stucco house on five acres, less than a mile from the Governor's residence. Illuminated fountain at the front, small lake at the back. Walled all around—all five acres. Mexican gardener and Filipina maid. Black cook from Charleston, South Carolina—so good the judge let her bring her husband; the children were old enough to take care of themselves.

A man was always at a desk in the lobby of the mansion, near a television monitor. He wore a fifteen round semiautomatic pistol at his side. Never smiled—not even for Judge Telamon. When he was off duty, another like him sat in the same place. There was a loaded Uzi submachine gun held by two clips under the desk, and two full magazines for the gun, in the drawer.

The cook's husband helped Morton take his duffel bag upstairs to his room. The maid followed to ask whether the room was satisfactory. It was filled with heavy mahogany furniture, and smelled of lemon oil. Morton shook his head. "It's perfect." If anything was unsatisfactory, he could not tell. This was the sort of luxury he had not even bothered to dream about.

"Judge Telamon wants you to come down to the library when you're done here," Mr. Mountrie, the cook's husband said.

The judge was waiting in the library. "When you're ready, I can have somebody take you to your home to get the rest of your things."

Morton shook his head. "I can't go back there, sir."

"I understand. We'll have to get you some new clothes and things then. As I said, when you're ready."

"Thank you, sir." Morton looked around the room filled from floor to ceiling with books on three walls.

"Do you have a favorite reading subject, Morton?" Telamon asked.

"I like poetry, sir. Good poetry. And the English classics."

"Favorite poets?"

"The English and Irish, sir. Some French and Spanish."

"American?" the judge asked.

"Frost and Whitman."

"No modern poets?"

"Oh, I read them, but there's no joy in their writing, no ecstasy in their language…too preoccupied with polemics."

"Don't you think poetry should be used in expressing points of view? For persuasion?"

"Yes, sir. But it must persuade with subtlety and conviction…and beauty; not beg for applause; or throw itself at me. Poetry should be used to excite all the senses…not just serve as a medium for discontent…or concealment of literary inadequacy."

"Lord have mercy, you sound older than me. Aren't you sixteen?"

"Yes, sir. I'll be seventeen in two months."

"Sixteen. And he sounds like a sixty-one year old. Any hobbies?"

"Karate, sir."

"Did your parents read a lot?"

"They used to read to me when I was a baby. They stopped when I learned to read for myself. Didn't read much themselves. Just magazines. Sometimes my mother read romance novels. But they encouraged me. Gave me book certificates as presents."

"Many friends?"

"Not many, usually older."

"Not surprised. Anyway, my wife was an avid reader and book collector; bought most of the books here. You'll probably find enough poetry here. She used to have readings in here when I was away. And I was away quite a lot." He looked around the room, then back at Morton. "I had hoped my home could provide a sufficiently stimulating environment for you. Now, I'm not so sure."

"I am not very demanding, sir. I can always find enough to keep me busy."

"Anything I can do for you now?"

"One important thing, sir. I would like to find the men who killed my parents."

Judge Telamon was unable to suppress the sudden jerk of his body. He could not have prepared himself for that one. He went to a chair. When he spoke, his voice had lost some of its sharpness. "Find your parents' killers? How am I going to do that, Morton? That's a job for the police."

"Yes, sir. I'm sorry."

August Telamon stared at him until they both looked away uncomfortably. "I suspect there's only one like you in the world," he said. "At least, I hope so."

There was a knock on the door, and the cook's husband looked in. "Dinner's ready Judge, sir."

"Thank you, Mr. Mountrie," he said, and turned to Morton. "Mrs. Mountrie's cooking is daily cause for celebration...and my most serious problem...forces me to exercise daily. And her bread pudding—always a topic of long discussion and admiration. She makes a secret bourbon sauce that makes people sneak into the kitchen to spy on her...stuff's so good. Know she won't even tell me how she makes it? Unfortunately, you'll have to wait until a special occasion for it."

They went into the smaller of the two dining rooms. "Mrs. Mountrie, this is our house guest, Mr. Morton Dirk. Mr. Dirk, Mrs. Mountrie. So, what are we having tonight, Ma'am?"

"Coq-au-vin, wild rice, watercress salad...and...bread pudding, Judge," Mrs. Mountrie said.

Judge Telamon's eyes widened in surprise. "No! And I was just telling Mr. Dirk about your bread pudding." he said.

Mrs. Mountrie was very pleased.

After dinner, Telamon leaned back in his chair. "This is the time for a glass of port and a cigar. But I don't smoke or drink. Sometimes a little wine before I eat. I find alcohol interferes with my memory. And I don't like to forget what I said. More bread pudding, Morton?"

"Yes, please. Best thing I ever ate."

"Me too."

Mrs. Mountrie beamed. Dirk Morton could have all the bread pudding he could eat.

Morton slept soundly that night. Could not remember his dreams when he awoke. He was satisfied with his first step.

The next morning, Mr. Mountrie knocked on his door at seven-thirty. "Mornin'. Judge said he'd be back at eight tonight. Said you have the run of the house. Said you should go out an' get some sunshine. If you want, I can show you around...but not the judge's bedroom. Ain't locked, but only the maid goes in to clean. Wouldn't go in if I was you."

"Okay, thanks. I'll be down in a little while. Tell Mrs. Mountrie I can make my own breakfast...please."

Mr. Mountrie frowned. "My wife don't let other people cook in her kitchen…and I know my wife better than you. If I was you, I'd wait until she was away…then clean up really good. Why you want to make your own breakfast, anyway?"

"Guess I'd better take your advice. Thanks," Morton said.

"See you downstairs."

That night, after a supper of bouillabaisse, Judge Telamon asked. "Did you have plans for college?"

"Yes, sir. I've applied to Emory, Harvard, Princeton, Yale…."

Telamon interrupted. "Only Ivy league? Did your parents have the resources?"

"No, sir. I had applied for scholarships."

"Morton, you do have an enormous amount of self-confidence, don't you?"

"My grades are good enough, sir. I've been a first honor's student. Consistently," Morton said.

"Yes, I'm sure. "And what did you plan to major in? Medicine?"

"No, sir. Literature."

The judge was silent for a minute. Kept his eyes on the floor. "Listen, Morton. What's a bright young black man going to do with a degree in literature? Who's going to employ you?"

"I want to teach, sir," Morton answered.

"Where?" Judge Telamon asked.

"Small college," Morton said.

"What's going on here, Morton Dirk? Are you making fun of me?"

"Never, sir. I want to study literature because I want to learn language well enough to persuade. Mastery of language is the key to power, sir."

"What power?"

"Control, sir?"

"You're losing me here, Morton.

"I'm sorry, sir. You must be wondering whether I know what I'm talking about. As you said, I'm only sixteen…."

"'Going on seventeen,'" the judge said. "But go on, please."

Morton smiled, so briefly, that Telamon was not sure that he had.

"Look at you for example. When I was in the safe house, I noticed how the police reacted to your name. They would have kissed your bottom if you had presented it. The immediate question I asked myself—and the policemen must have asked themselves too—why me? A nobody; parents killed in a hit; parents associated with crooks. The only thing I have going for me is that I'm a high achiever, and unconventional in other ways. I believe you have taken me into your home—at some risk to yourself—because you have some plan for me."

August Telamon opened his mouth to speak, but Morton continued quickly.

"I do not have much going for me, now…and it will be difficult for me to prove myself on my own. So, I need a guardian, or a champion. You need some skill or promise that you have seen in me. I am satisfied with that. If you help me with my education, I'll do whatever you want. We're very similar, I suspect, Judge Telamon. I'm sure that you started out like me…a nobody…invisible. And as you've found out, power can compensate for all previous humiliations. Power is its own reward."

"What kind of power are you looking for, Morton?"

"The ultimate, sir."

"Power to murder somebody?"

"Murder is destruction of life, sir, that's not power. Any loser with a gun can do that. But to be able to end life at a precise time and place, and by a precise means, all of one's choosing. That…is power."

"You want to be a killer, Morton Dirk?"

"No, sir. But I want to have that kind of power."

"Why?" Telamon asked.

"So no one will ever be able to walk into my bedroom at a time of his own choosing, and blow my brains out, and with the arrogance that would leave a family member alive…especially a child."

"So, how should I help you?"

"Help me get a good education. A superb education."

"And what do I get in return?"

"The best."

"Of what?"

"Of what you have in mind for me," Morton replied.

August Telamon rose, his face a little paler than it was during dinner. "I usually read until ten or so…down here. But tonight I think I'll go to bed a little early. I cannot recall a similar experience with anyone, especially one so young. And I have to contend with some supremely intelligent people—a lot of them on the wrong side of the bench, too. But no one like you. You've overwhelmed and exhausted me…mentally. But we must talk again…and I'd like you to meet a couple of my close friends. I think they'd enjoy a discussion with you. Goodnight, Mr. Dirk….Damn'. Now, you've got me forgetting you're not my age. Goodnight, Morton."

"Goodnight, sir," Morton said.

Judge Telamon sat at his desk, with his hand resting on the telephone for several minutes, trying to control his breathing. He mopped the sweat from his face and neck several times, although the room temperature was kept at seventy degrees. When he felt in control, he dialed a number.

A voice said, "Yes?"

He asked for another number. Waited. An uninflected, disinterested voice asked, "Reason for your call?"

"John Milton," Telamon replied.

There was a pause, and Telamon heard the sounds of electronic switches. Then….

"Paradise Lost?" another voice asked. It sounded like breaking glass.

"Paradise Found," Telamon said.

The tone of the voice changed. Grew warmer. "Congratulations. You still are the best."

Telamon laughed. "Not any more. I just found the best."

"How many years?"

"Eight, I'd say...at the most."

"We can wait," the voice said.

"And I'd like you to meet him," Telamon said.

"When? Are you that confident?"

"I am. And he will never have to see you again. In two weeks?"

"Not yet, but I shall call the others," the voice said. "They will come."

Telamon put down the telephone, and as he had seen the younger lawyers in his court do, pumped his right hand down. Hard. "Yes."

The next morning, when Judge Telamon went down to breakfast, he found Morton listening earnestly to Mrs. Mountrie as she described how she made her famous bread pudding. She stopped when the judge came in. He pretended not to have heard. "Morning all, slept well?

"Good morning, sir. Very well, sir."

"Good morning, Judge," Mrs. Mountrie said. "Fruit and cereal, today."

When they were done, he handed Morton a business card. "Mr. Mountrie will take you to Nieman Marcus after lunch. Ask for this gentleman in the men's. Tell him who you are. He'll help you pick out some clothes and a couple of suits. Tell him you must have any alterations done by Friday after next. We're having some special old business friends of mine over for dinner. And we usually dress up a bit for these occasions. I'm sorry, but we're still a little old fashioned about some things…. Anyway, I think you'll enjoy their company. And I know they will enjoy yours."

"Yes, sir," Morton said.

Two weeks late, on Sunday evening, at precisely seven o'clock, a black Lincoln Town Car with darkened windows drove through the gate to August Telamon's home, continued up the drive past the right side of the house, and parked at the back. A second, identical car followed two minutes later. The guard locked the gate behind them. The driver of the first car was just five feet tall, with delicate features that made him resemble a finely molded chocolate doll with an expression of great amusement.

He wore a black suit. Judge August Telamon waited for him just outside the back door.

"Augustus," the smaller man said. "Very, very anticipated.

"Hadrian," Telamon replied, "worth the wait."

The driver of the driver of the second car was over six feet tall, wiry, and very dark. He walked with the delicacy and deliberation of a cat. The thin oval of his face reflected no emotion. He also wore black. "Hadrian. Augustus," he said.

"Galba," they greeted him.

"So, Augustus. I hear that this prodigy of yours surpasses the reports that came back from our searches," Hadrian said.

"You will see for yourself," Telamon said, "but it is as if the boy were manufactured according to specifications. In some ways, he's unnatural...his intelligence is frightening. He's not aggressive, but very perspicacious. Be careful not to be deliberately deceptive...he will know."

"The potential, the potential," Galba said.

"How many like him have we found this year?" Hadrian asked Telamon.

"One. Two good prospects identified...one male, one female...but still young...juniors in high school."

"Enough?" Hadrian asked.

"Quite. One more than necessary," Telamon answered.

They preceded Telamon inside, into the library. The table was laden with a selection of fruits and vegetables, cheeses, sliced roast chicken, lamb, salmon, and sliced French bread. There were three glass decanters filled with fruit juices and a dusty bottle of port with a faded label.

Morton Dirk was standing near the table waiting. His hands clasped behind his back. He was nervous, but his hands were dry. The newcomers went directly to him. "Mr. Dirk, so pleased to meet you after all the good things we had heard. I'm Peter Hall," said Hadrian.

"And I'm Charles John," said Galba.

"Two of the greatest intellects you will ever meet," Telamon said.

"Only when Augustus Telamon dies," Galba said.

"I am sorry if I appear nervous, sirs, but this is a completely new experience for me. You must know that Judge Telamon has been the only miracle I have ever experienced. And I am desperately trying not to disappoint him."

"Very well said, Mr. Dirk," Hadrian said, "Augustus, you must be flattered. You have awed a prodigy. Tell me, Mr. Dirk, did you speak like this at home, or at school, or to your acquaintances?"

"No sir...I translated."

"Well said, well said." Galba was almost giggling. His face shone with rare delight.

"Come, come, let us get something from the table and sit," Telamon said.

When they were seated, Hadrian pulled his chair closer to Morton. "I have had this question posed all week. Judge Telamon has told us of your definition of power. Tell me this: why does such a concept exist. Why should anyone need power. Can't society exist as a cooperative among equals? A true democracy?"

"That would be unnatural, sir. Even when all members of a community are equally skilled or capable, there are single decisions to be made that affect all; and these decisions could not have been conceived at the same time, and in the same form by all. Every great achievement had been created by one mind at one point in time."

"Some minds are superior to others?" Galba asked.

"Yes, sir," Morton said.

"Where do these superior minds come from? Accidents of nature? Good parents? Ethnicity?"

"Accidents, sir. They arise spontaneously. Otherwise we'd be all geniuses or all fools.

"And are these superior minds geniuses?" Hadrian asked.

"Not necessarily, sir. Many geniuses are incompetent in matters outside their genius. A superior mind is different: it knows how to control fools and geniuses."

"Tell me this," Galba said, "do you believe in a superior power—beyond our full understanding—that bestows these differences?"

"I do not believe so, sir. I believe the genetic dice are rolled, and a few will get multiple sixes. Most will not."

"How about you," Hadrian asked, "did you not inherit your intelligence from your parents?"

"My parents were not very intelligent people, Mr. Hall. In fact, their stupidity got them both murdered."

His parents: he had not thought of them since he left the protection of the police. Now, a few unbidden fragments: Sunday afternoon, his father giving his black shoes their weekly polish; his mother ironing a week's worth of blouses, skirts and dresses. Your homework ready for tomorrow? One was sure to ask. Then a joke...to be laughed at more loudly by the teller. Then the defeat of conversation by the noises from the television. Then bed. His parents saw him, heard him, but never discovered his world.

"I'm sorry," both visitors said.

"Thank you." Morton looked into the distance between the men.

Galba spoke first. "Let me pose the inevitable question: Judge Telamon has of course, already told us your answer. But tell us why you want study...literature."

Morton Dirk answered almost before Galba had finished speaking. "You know the Latin saying: *vox populi, vox dei*? The voice of the people is the voice of God? Well then sir, what if someone can convince others that *he* is the voice of God — the voice of the inevitable?"

"And how can the study of literature give that power?" Hadrian asked. "I'm sorry to be so blunt...but what on earth are you talking about?"

"Oh, it does not. What it does, is provide the material that this power will require. A piece of stone or wood does not create art. The creation comes from the artist using these raw materials. What I need, sirs, is access to the raw material of words."

There was a silence of several minutes as the three men stared at Morton. Their eyes unblinking, their lips taut. Galba spoke first. "Have you shared these thoughts or opinions with anyone else, Mr. Dirk?"

"No, sir. I had not dared until Judge Telamon took me in. He allowed me to speak. He encouraged me to, I should say. But these were thoughts that have been growing through much of my adolescence."

"Have you been popular with girls? Are you sexually active? Hadrian asked.

"I have had only two sexual experiences, sir. I would have enjoyed them better if I hadn't had to pay."

"Prostitutes?"

"No, sir. Neighbors. Girls do not find me sufficiently attractive. So…I had to pay them for their trouble. Most women do not seem to notice me. For that matter, people are unaware of my presence most of the time."

"Remarkable…most extraordinary thing I have ever heard," Hadrian said, "At this point gentlemen, what I need is a drink. Augustus, I noticed a bottle of port on the table. Do you have brandy anywhere? I need something more substantial right now."

Augustus Telamon went to a cupboard at the end of the room.

Hadrian continued, "Judge Telamon told us of your conversations, and your determination to pursue higher studies in literature. We, the three of us, are financially fortunate, and we are anxious to make you this offer: We will finance your education, at whatever institution, in any country that will accept you. We will provide a generous stipend. In return, we ask that you allow us to employ your talents on completion of your studies. We shall fund any postgraduate studies for you too, although I believe that would only mean supplementing the grants that any worthwhile institution would impress on you."

"Is that satisfactory, Mr. Dirk?" Galba asked.

"It is many times more than I would have dared hoped for, sirs. I am very grateful," Morton replied. At that moment, he wished his eyes were capable of forcing a tear.

"Augustus," Hadrian called, "we toast tonight. Pity you're too young to drink, Mr. Dirk."

"I've tried it, sir. It interferes with my memory."

Augustus Telamon laughed out loud; wagged his finger at Morton. "Now let us celebrate this rare get-together. Tell us, Morton, have you read Milton's Paradise Lost?"

"Some of it, sir."

"Any favorite passages?"

"Yes, sir," Morton replied, and began:

"A mind not to be changed by place or time.
The mind is its own place, and in itself
Can make a heav'n of hell, a hell of heav'n."
The three men applauded loudly. "We must speak again,"
Galba said, "I do not remember such an enjoy able evening."

"Yes, yes. Marvelous, marvelous." Hadrian kept shaking his head in wonder.

Judge Telamon beamed at Morton as if at a triumphant creation. And later, as the judge was seeing his guests to their cars, he asked: "Do you gentlemen agree that we have found a miracle? A sixteen year-old kid who can match wits with anyone of us…and probably best us. Damn."

Galba stood very still, and looked down at his shoes. Small twitches of his forehead overcoming his usual impurtability. He said: "I wonder whether he will do what we want; or whether we shall find ourselves doing what he wants."

"He will do exactly what we want, Galba, because we shall give him what he wants: The power to end life at a precise time and place, and by a precise means," Augustus Telamon said.

5

When Dirk Morton arrived in Cambridge, Massachusetts, to attend Harvard University, the days were warm enough to make his long excursions into the surrounding neighborhoods comfortable. No one took much notice of the quiet walker, or saw him stop and register landmarks, street names; or listen in on their conversations. Occasionally, another young black man would look briefly into his eyes and immediately forget his face: no challenge there. Just a nod. Sometimes, "What's happening?" No recollection or mention of his presence.

He liked the air of permanence exhaled by old brick buildings shouldering the narrow streets that cut through the city with formal disdain for right angles and logic. Each with its selfish color and architectural quirk, leaning on black wrought-iron arms that enclosed steps zigzagging up and down to foyers and basements.

And he was the quiet shadow on the Harvard campus and in the halls and classrooms. His classmates were aware of his presence and his brilliance in the classroom, but after the lecture…no one felt the compulsion or necessity to get closer. Not actual discomfort with him. Just a vague uneasiness.

No membership in any student associations or participation in activities.

The staff at the Peabody Museum no longer stared curiously at the black wraith who came to examine the geological and paleontological specimens. Almost every day, looking intensely at models of the earth's crust; three-dimensional depictions of the continents and the ocean floor; bones and casts of bones; painted dioramas.

Two or three times, someone had stopped and tried to draw him into conversation. The usual tentative inquiry: "Geology student?"

"No."

"Oh."

"Just looking."

"What's your major?"

"English Literature."

"Oh." Without understanding. "See you around."

"Yes."

One week after his arrival in Boston, at the end of a telephone conversation, Judge Telamon asked: "Still involved with your karate?"

"Haven't joined a dojo yet," Morton answered.

"Got a name and a number here for you. Give them a call. They come highly recommended."

After the call, Morton looked in the Yellow Pages of the telephone directory. No listing for the name. He called.

"May I speak with Mr. Saul Yura?"

"Minute, please," a woman's voice said.

Then, "Saul Yura."

"My name is Morton Dirk. Your dojo was recommended to me by...."

"Yes, Mr. Dirk. When can you come? Do you need directions?"

"Please. Tomorrow. Seven?"

"Seven o'clock. Goodbye, sir."

'Mr. Dirk'...and 'sir.' No 'Morton.'

There was no sign at the address he was given. He knocked on a green-painted door. A tiny Japanese lady in an exquisite white silk kimono let him in. Her bowed head did not allow him to see her face. She pointed to the door at the opposite side of a sitting room with four black-lacquered chairs arranged symmetrically around a circular matching table. Morton opened the door to stairs leading down. Saul Yura waited at the bottom of the stairs. He was taller than Morton had expected, well over six feet, and older. He seemed about sixty. His hand felt as hard as marble. "I assume that you know little about this dojo. Your fees have been paid in advance. We would be happy if you could come every three days, but we know you have other…important matters. I assume also that you have some skill in defensive karate. Here, we teach you how to overcome an opponent's defenses. Our karate is not for amateurs, or for tournaments. You understand, of course?"

"Quite," Morton said. Telamon was thorough.

Yura handed Morton the white doji that was draped over his left arm—with a white belt.

"I have a black belt," Morton said.

"Not here. Not yet," Yura said. He pointed to a curtained alcove. "Change please."

There were no introductions to the six men and five women who trained with him. And none of the bows or other formalities associated with the sport. There were no colored belts.

It would be three years before Yura handed Morton a black doji. "We don't need black belts," he would say.

Two months before he left for Atlanta at the end of his last undergraduate year, he had his first date: She sat behind him in two of their classes. One Friday evening in October, as he headed for the bus stop, she ran to catch up with him. "Hey there. My name's Georgia. Mind if I walk with you?"

"No…pleasure," Morton said.

"Keep to yourself a lot, don't you?"

"Conspicuous?" Morton asked.

"Yeah, sure. Never seen you talk to anyone in class. Always by yourself. Shy?"

"Guess so."

"Bad experience with a woman?" she asked.

"No...not at all. Guess I don't have good people skills. What's your name? Mine's Morton Dirk...Atlanta, Georgia."

"That's my name too..." she said. "Georgia Enoch...New York. Noo Yawk, if you prefer." Looked up at his face. "Shoot, I almost made you smile."

"If I asked you out...would you come?" Morton asked.

"That was quick for a shy guy. Sure. Here's my number. Call if you have a good idea. I like old black and white movies and the symphony."

"Tonight, too early?" he asked.

"Gosh, it must be a long time since...for you," she said.

"I'm sorry," he said.

"No problemo," she said. "Not that it's been any better for me. Why don't you come over...just for a chat, now? Eight's a good time. But you've got to leave by ten. Okay?"

Morton stopped to look at her walk away. Athletic, about five foot eight, appeared to glide over the ground. Hair cut in a close Afro. Eyes strongly slanted. Small, very pointed breasts and a bottom slightly too large for a fashion runway.

The following Friday, Morton took her to Symphony Hall. Afterwards, in a taxi back to her apartment, she asked, "Want to stay the night?"

"Of course, I would," he said.

A short time later, as she was hanging up their coats, she asked, "Know I wasn't wearing any underwear at the symphony?"

"Good thing I didn't...or I wouldn't have heard a note," he said.

"Want to see?" she asked.

She made him sit still on the bed while she removed all her clothes and pirouetted slowly.

"This is cruel," Morton said.

"I know," Georgia replied. "Now it's your turn. Take all your clothes off. I want to see you…in all your…embarrassment." She made him stand close to her face. When she was satisfied, she asked: "You think you can manage to stay the night without wanting too much?"

"If that's what you want," Morton answered.

"For now…yes. I don't mind holding and cuddling…but no sex. Okay?" Georgia said.

"I assume that one day…all will be revealed,"

"One day you'll be able to have as much as you can manage."

"Is this a: 'wait until we get to know each other better?'"

"Sort of. I'm going to ask you something very personal…when was the last time you had sex?"

"Couple months ago. And I didn't care for a repeat. Neither of us had much enthusiasm. Did it, I suppose, because it was the thing to do after a couple of dates."

"Still seeing her?" Georgia asked.

"No. It was not special enough to want more. Mutual."

"Want to see me again?"

"Yes," Morton said.

"Why?"

"Curiosity…and…."

"And?"

"I'm not very experienced sexually," Morton replied.

"Do you think you could handle a long-term relationship that was very sexual, but had no emotional commitment?"

"I'm not looking for a wife. I'm only twenty-one."

"Exactly. I couldn't deal with emotional immaturity."

"I didn't ask for a commitment from you…. How old are you, Georgia?"

"Twenty-five," she said.

"Why would you be interested in a…kid?"

"There's something special about you, Morton Dirk. Special…like weird. And I like excitement. By the way, I'm no innocent."

"You practice witchcraft, you're about to tell me?"

"Nah, nothing that banal. I used to be a prostitute…for three years. That's why I'm a little old for an undergraduate. I was one of the best in Manhattan." She looked intently at his face.

Morton's face remained impassive. "You obviously know much more about sex than I do then. Should have a lot to teach."

"Now, are you still sure you want to see me," Georgia asked.

"Long-term," he replied.

That night, she slept with an arm around his shoulders, but pulled away whenever he rolled against her. The next morning, as she walked him to the train station, she asked: "Have you ever lost control? You know…of your temper, or emotions? I was expecting you to try all night to get into me…and you just went to sleep. You're a cold bastard, aren't you?"

"Isn't that what you wanted?"

"Yes, but…you could have tried," she said.

"I don't play games, Georgia Enoch," Morton replied.

"So, are we getting together again…even if you don't get any?"

"Definitely, Georgia Enoch. I love a good mystery. Let's talk again, soon."

"This is going to be fun," she said.

"Listen, what made you 'one of the best…in Manhattan?'" Morton asked, when they were at the station entrance.

"Whatever I do, I do extremely well. Like you. Never had less than an A-plus grade in College. Like you."

"How did you know that?" he asked.

"People talk.… See you soon, Morton."

Morton slept with Georgia Enoch one night a week for a month without any sexual contact. Then early one morning, he returned from the bathroom to find her naked under the sheets. "Take your clothes off," she said. She played over his body with her fingers and tongue until he was close to tears.

"Please?" he asked.

She pulled him over to lie on her. "It's all yours now," she said, "Do what ever you like."

And every week, she led him to a new erotic discovery; leaving him so sated that he lost all interest in other women.

But no words of endearment, putting her hand over his mouth when she sensed his attempt to be sentimental. "None of this, 'I love you,' stuff. Remember? All I want from you is sex…all you can give. And what you're getting from me is better than you can get anywhere else…for love or money."

Georgia Enoch was the only woman he saw for the rest of his last term. "I'm coming back to Harvard for grad school next year," he told her.

"I'm staying in Boston, she said. Got an offer with a computer firm to write software programs. I'll take the job if you're coming back. Want to stay close to you,"

"Serious?"

"Yes," Georgia said, "Going to see some folks in New York for a couple of weeks. Then coming back. Should be starting in August. But we'll keep in touch?"

"Of course. Think you could make it to Atlanta?" Morton asked.

She shook her head. "Don't think so…too much to take care of. But thanks. Someday."

Three months later, she was waiting when he arrived at Logan Airport. "Got a nice new place…air conditioning and all," she said. And I bought me a new expensive car—five year old VW Beetle. But it moves. Missed me?"

"Celibacy is very unfulfilling," Morton said.

"Liar. Didn't have any while you were in Atlanta? Not once?" Georgia asked.

"Not once, I swear."

"You're not natural," she said.

"How about you?" Morton asked.

"Not once."

"Liar," he said.

"No, honestly. Now, let's get home and put on Ravel's Bolero. And you can work out all your frustrations and deprivations. Want to see how much you've remembered," she said. "Then I'll cook you a nice dinner. And afterwards we'll start all over again."

"Best teacher I've ever had," Morton said.

"And we've only just started," Georgia Enoch said.

One night, after they had returned from the cinema, Morton said, "Georgia, will you tell me something more about yourself? How did you go from what you told me you were...from hooker to Harvard Honors graduate?"

"Oh, the usual: single mother, inner-city neighborhood, peer pressure, low self-esteem, etcetera." Georgia paused, and laughed. "I'm joking. I came from a good upper middle-class family. Both parents professors at Cornell. I was a reluctant virgin until twelfth grade. Had a French teacher from the Caribbean whom I had the worst crush on...and I was too headstrong to even think of hiding my availability. He picked up quickly on it, and invited me to come to his apartment one Saturday. You can imagine much of the rest. He introduced me to good music and food and the arts. My parents are sophisticated folks...but always too busy. He also taught me things about my body that weren't in any book I had read. Things I had never even heard the other kids talk about. After that, I couldn't go out with any guy my age. Then he began to pay me. Don't know why, but I took the money...and liked it. At least one hundred dollars each time I slept with him. Then he introduced me to a friend...told me the friend would pay two hundred dollars to sleep with me. The friend paid three hundred for what I gave him. Then more friends. In one year, I had become a rich high-class whore. Decided not to go on to college. Hell, I could have retired in five more years, with the money I was making. Left home and got my own apartment in Manhattan. Bought me a black Alpha Romeo coupe.

"Then one night, on the way back from entertaining two rich new clients, I got lost. Stopped to ask a guy in some sort of uniform for directions, and found an enormous stainless steel penis stuck in my face. Biggest gun I had ever seen. Guy got into my car, made me drive to an overpass and raped me. Bastard had such a good time, he got careless...he thought I was enjoying it. Actually put the gun down on the back seat. I clamped my legs around his waist and gave him such an orgasm. He didn't know where he was. Started calling me, 'baby, darling, lover doll.' Even closed his eyes when I asked him to. I rolled him over to the right, jammed him against the door, and grabbed the gun. Made him get out of the car. He was standing naked near the car, grinning, still thinking we were friends...until I shot him in the balls. And while he was lying on the ground screaming, I shot him in the belly, then emptied the gun in his body. Eventually, I found my way out of there. Threw the gun into the East River. First time I had ever touched a gun. It was much heavier than I had expected...and it almost tore my hand off every time I fired. I had to use both hands.

"I was sick for a week. Then went to the doctor. I was infected with gonorrhea...and crab lice Eventually, I told my friend about it...asked him whether I should turn myself in to the police. He said no. A week later, he asked me how I felt about the killing. Told him I didn't feel anything...it had been like getting rid of garbage. That was when he suggested I go to college. Said he saw a rare potential in me. My parents were only too happy to pay for college. I had no trouble getting into Harvard, although my parents wanted me to apply to Cornell...where they could have kept an eye on me, I suppose."

"What happened to your teacher friend?" Morton asked.

"Saw him a couple times during my first year. Came to Boston to visit me. Then he disappeared. Never a word again. And here I am, being laid by a teenager...and enjoying it."

"And the police?" Morton asked.

"Nothing. Didn't even hear about it on the news."

"Do you miss your old life?"

"No. Got all I need now. And things are too dangerous out there," Georgia Enoch said. A little later, she said, "But I did enjoy the sex. I've got to behave now…but I could have sex every day for the rest of my life."

"I'm a little jealous…you've had a much more interesting life than mine," he said.

"For now," she said. "Want to make love?"

"Very much," he replied.

When they were done, Georgia asked, "Do you think you could kill a person, Morton?"

"In self-defense?" he asked.

"No. If that person were an obstacle…to something you wanted very much."

"Yes, I could," Morton said, and waited for the expression of concern.

There was a faint smile on her lips—like relief. "We'll see. Want me to fix us dinner?" Georgia asked.

"No, let me take you out," Morton said. "Wouldn't mind spaghetti and meatballs and garlic bread."

"Me too…then we can breathe on each other," Georgia said.

At dinner she asked him, "Tell me some more about yourself, Morton."

"Parents killed by an intruder; was adopted by a judge; no distinguishing traits. That's my life."

"What turns you on, Morton. Apart from sex?" she asked.

"Literature and geology…and you," he answered.

"I know about the last, I don't understand the first two."

"Language gives one the skill to control others. And geology is the study of the greatest forces on our planet. Both are about power."

"Smartass," Georgia said.

"I'm learning from you," Morton said.

"I know a more powerful force than language," she said.

"What? Sex?"

"Right."

"Smartass." Morton said.

"Ready to make love again?" Georgia asked.

"Give me fifteen minutes…you make me do most of the work," Morton said.

"Smartass," she said.

One Sunday evening, they were watching the television program *Sixty Minutes*, when Morton rose suddenly from the couch and turned the television off. He pulled a chair closer to the couch, and sat facing Georgia. "Okay, what were they talking about just now on the program?" he asked.

"Don't remember…something about…." she replied.

"Come on, what's bothering you?" Morton asked. He knew she would tell him. She was searching for a way to begin: to make him responsible for her telling.

"Remember what I asked you…about killing somebody?" Georgia asked.

"Sure. You want me to kill somebody for you?" He started smiling. Stopped when she nodded.

"Are you serious?" he asked.

"I've got to help a friend…or she's going to get killed," Georgia answered. "I was going to do it myself."

"Better tell me what's going on. What if you got caught? What if…a thousand things? I assume it involves a man," Morton said.

"A friend…a very close friend…asked me to help her get away from her husband. He's been beating her ever since she decided to go back to school. She's a lab technician at the University Hospital. Got accepted into a Master's program, and her husband couldn't handle it. He says she didn't discuss it, or ask him. Juvenile stuff. Looks like he's afraid she's going to make him look bad."

"What does he do?"

"Policeman. Never went to college."

"So why doesn't she walk out?" Morton asked.

"First thing a man asks," Georgia said. "He'd find her. And the law doesn't give much protection to battered women. A lot of them get killed when they walk away. Then the law steps in...and he's a cop."

"Why do you want to get involved?"

"Because it was I who persuaded her to go to graduate school."

"Any children?" he asked.

"Miscarried. After one of his beatings," Georgia said.

"And how do I help?" Morton asked.

"Got to think about it," she said.

"Yes, we'd better."

"Would you help me if you were certain we could get away with it?" she asked.

"I wouldn't do it if I thought we'd get caught," he answered. "Thought of a plan?"

"It needs two people. I'd be the bait...you'd come to help me when he got violent," Georgia said.

"Then we call the police and tell them I stepped in to help a lady in distress?"

"No. We walk away. Forget the whole thing. His wife will find out when the paper reports the discovery of the body," she said.

"Let's hear what you've got," Morton said.

That night in bed, she turned toward him. "Morton, hold me very tight until I fall asleep."

"Going soft on me?" he asked.

"Shut up, and hold me," she replied.

The following Friday afternoon, Geogia called the police precinct from a pay telephone. "Sergeant Leray Belvedere," she said.

She was put on hold for almost two minutes, then: "Sergeant Belvedere," the baritone voice said.

"Hi, Sarge," she said, "if you got to hit on a woman, why don't you get on who can take it?"

"Who the hell is this?" Belvedere asked. But his voice remained calm.

"I work at the University Hospital. Ain't enough makeup to hide the bruises on your wife's face. And don't ask who I am. You know I won't tell you. And I'm calling from a pay telephone, so I'm not going to chat with you until you put a trace on me. I'll call you again. Bye, darling."

She called the next Wednesday, but he was not in. She contacted him on Thursday afternoon. "I've been thinking of you all week," she said. "I like a little spice with my sex…I like a man who knows how to handle his woman. As long as I don't show the bruises. Think you can handle this bitch?"

"You're looking for serious trouble, lady. I don't abuse my wife. And right now, you're in dangerous territory," Belvedere said.

But Georgia could hear his breathlessness. He would be looking forward to her next call. She called two weeks later. "Want to get together, hunk?" she asked when he picked up the telephone.

"Yes, to place your ass under arrest," he replied.

"Goodbye then. Looks like you're afraid to handle a real woman. And I'm the best you'll ever put your eyes on. I'm a real fine woman, Sarge. So long. You probably couldn't handle a piece like me, anyway."

"Wait, wait, wait," he said. "I'm interested. Where?"

"Someplace safe for me, I can tell you that. I don't trust your ass one bit. How do I know you won't arrest me?"

"For what?" he asked.

"I don't know. You'd think of something," Georgia answered.

"Anyway, let me think of something and call you next week. But you got to come immediately after I call. I'm not giving you time to set me up."

"That's cool," Belvedere answered, "pick your place…I'm interested, I told you."

"See you soon, lover. I think we can get something really hot going. Just as long as you don't lose control. When I'm done with you, you're going to want to kiss my butt. Won't be able to stop saying thanks."

"Mean that?" he asked.

"You be a good boy, and I'll send you to heaven. Best you'll ever have in your life," she said.

It was two weeks before she called again.

"Thought you had forgotten me," Leray Belvedere said.

"No, dear heart," Georgia said. "Been looking for a good place...where we wouldn't be disturbed. Wouldn't want some of your coworkers sneaking up on us."

"Don't worry about that. Let's just get together for a chat. See if we're okay with each other...comfortable," he said.

"Fair enough," she replied. "How about Hyde Park, near the Neponser River. Riverbanks are romantic."

"You serious about this?" he asked.

"Sure. Your wife's a good-looking lady. So I know she must have married a fine looking man. Now, remember. I don't want you to touch me with anything but your hand. Okay?"

"Okay, baby. You got it," Belvedere said. "Want me to bring anything?"

"Just yourself," Georgia answered. "Want you all hot and bothered."

Leray Belvedere encountered only five people in the park on his way to the river bank: Two male joggers, an elderly couple, and a female jogger. Half a mile away, there was a man feeding ducks in a pond. Looked black—could have been the distance. Leray was five foot ten, stocky, and well-muscled. He was thirty five, but looked twenty one. Good looking; and the thin, precise mustache helped.

The woman was standing on the riverbank, exactly where she had said. She had a bottom that looked even better than he had imagined. There was nobody on the opposite bank. Enough trees and shrubs on their side to hide them. He had bought a packet containing three condoms on the way to the park. Intended to make all the use he could, of the two hours he had. Not too rough. If this woman was good, his wife could do all the degrees she wanted. He could hardly control his breathing. Could already feel the sting on his hand as he slapped that butt. Not too hard. Go easy first time. Unless it looked like there wasn't going to be a second time.

"Hey there," he called, "waiting for somebody?"

Georgia turned. "Who are you?" she asked.

"Sergeant Belvedere," he said.

"Hello, Sarge…you're better looking than I had thought," she said.

"And you're a very fine lady. Yes, indeed," he answered.

"So, what you got in mind?" she asked.

"Got two hours. Thought we could get to know each other."

"Brought anybody with you?" she asked.

"Nah. Told you I was coming alone."

"Want to get acquainted…out here in the open?" she asked.

He looked around. "Don't see anybody, but it may be safer in the there." He pointed to a small copse.

"Come sit down here for a minute." She sat down and patted the ground on her left.

Belvedere sat down. Georgia ran her hand up the inside of his legs. "Checking to see if you had handcuffs or a gun." She stopped at his crotch. "Man, that's a big gun…bet you can shoot that good."

His voice was hoarse. "Let's get in there, baby. Can't hold on."

She followed him into the trees. "You go first," she said.

"No. We go together," he said. "Shirts first."

They both undid their shirts. Shoes. Unbuckled their pants. She sat down to pull her pants off. She undid her brassiere. He leaned against a tree to pull his pants off. She was naked when he turned to her. He ripped a hole below the waistband of his briefs as he tore them off.

She turned her back to him, put both hands against a tree, and leaned her head on her hands. "Ready," she said.

He pulled his belt from his pants. Stood behind her staring at her buttocks. "Sweetest thing I ever seen. So help me," he said. Brought the belt down hard across her bottom. Saw her muscles tighten.

"More," she said.

He hit her twice more.

"Now," she said, turning toward him. Tears ran down her cheeks. "Lie on the ground," she said.

He shook his head. "Want you down on hands and knees, bitch," he said.

She knelt and placed her hands on the ground. She felt his hands circle her thighs, then move back to open her with his thumbs. She rolled to the left, on her back, and her let kicked out hard—toward his groin.

He was too fast. Spun to his left. Kicked her hard on her extended ankle. She felt an electric jolt up her leg, and knew she was finished. Waited. Belvedere stood over her. The belt was wrapped around his right hand, with the large brass buckle dangling. "When I'm finished with you, not even the hospital's gonna be able to help you," he said. He raised his arm high.

Morton's heel hit him at the base of his skull. Georgia heard the firecracker snaps of Belvedere's cervical vertebrae as they shattered. The policeman's body fell across her. He lay very still. Morton rolled the body off her.

"Broke my ankle...I think," she said.

He helped her up, and she leaned against a pine tree. Picked up her clothes and helped her dress. "Better hurry," he said, "you're turning me on like nobody's business."

Georgia sat back down to put her shoes on. "Damn', just look at my foot." Her right ankle and foot were swollen, and the skin broken where Belvedere's foot had caught her. She tried to walk, and screamed. Fell to the ground again. "Can't walk, Morton...and the car's about a mile away."

"It's okay," he said, "I'll get you there if I have to carry you. But we've got to get out of here." He put his left arm around her waist. "Put your right arm around my neck...let's go. Don't forget your shoe."

At the emergency room at the hospital, she said that she had been playing soccer. It was three hours before they got home.

The morning news at six the next day began with the report of Sergeant Leray Belvedere's death. The precinct captain was confident they would have the killer or killers before the week was out.

After the newscast, Georgia asked, "How do you feel?" she asked.

"Fine,"

"I mean about Belvedere," she said.

"Oh. Like taking out the garbage," he said.

"You're a cold bastard," she said.

"What about you?" he asked

"Wet and horny. Come here. Watch my foot."

Two years later, Georgia Enoch vanished. No one at her firm or at her apartment could help Morton. There was no forwarding address for her anywhere. No telephone listing for her in New York City, or in Boston. He had anticipated her disappearance. What surprised him was how much he missed her.

It was as he had always suspected: Saul Yura—took care of his physical condition. Georgia Enoch—took care of his sexual needs…with no involvement. Telamon and his pals had probably listened to every grunt he had made in Georgia's bed.

One week after Georgia's disappearance, a fellow graduate student accepted Morton's invitation to dinner. She followed him around his kitchen as he washed four chicken breasts in lemon juice, then rubbed them with sea salt, thyme, garlic, and black pepper. Put them on the counter top to sit for an hour; then dusted the pieces lightly with flour and browned them in hot olive oil in a cast-iron frying pan. When that was done, he removed the chicken and put in a handful of chopped red peppers, tomatoes, white and green onions, and chives; stirred in some red wine to dissolve the caramelized flour. The kitchen filled with smells that made Julietta Samms want to move in with Morton. He put the chicken breasts back into the browned vegetables, added a handful of peeled baby carrots, stirred them together and poured a cup of burgundy into the pan. Covered it and turned the flame down. "Should be done in half an hour," he said. Put another pan on the stove, and poured in rice and water; peeled russet potatoes, water, and a little salt in a third pan. "Want to help with the salad?" he asked.

"Please, I'm beginning to feel really useless, here," Julietta said.

"In the 'fridge. Take out what you'd like. Drink? There's a Riesling in there too…if you don't mind that."

She slept over that night. Explained that her boyfriend worked on an oilfield in Alaska; and she was not interested in another commitment. But she did not mind visiting Morton every now and then…first guy she had met who could really cook. And…that was the best sex she had ever had. "I'm really sorry that we didn't meet earlier," she said.

He agreed. "Just my luck. All the best ones already taken."

The following week, she accepted from him a gift certificate for a year's service for her six-year-old Subaru at a nearby dealership.

After Julietta Samms, there were two female students from classes that he taught as an instructor in English poetry. It was all very discreet. Morton stopped thinking of Georgia Enoch.

And he beat Galba's prediction by one year—completed his studies in less than eight years.

Seven years after Morton had left Atlanta, Judge Telamon told his household staff that Morton would be home in a week. "And he's coming back as 'Doctor Dirk.' Got his doctorate in English Literature."

The staff looked at each other, wondering what that smart young black man was going to do for a living. For the next two weeks, he rose early to practice Spanish with the gardener. He spent the afternoons on the Metropolitan Atlanta Transit Authority, riding the buses and trains until he thought he could find his way home from most of central Atlanta without asking for directions. No one bothered to look twice at his face, and would probably not remember more about him than making room for another passenger. Face and clothes less interesting than the next person entering or rising to leave; less interesting than happenstance on the sidewalks on inside the cars keeping pace with the bus.

He spoke only to excuse himself into the aisle, when he thought he had traveled far enough; or to evade the eagerness of another for conversation. His eyes intent on narrow streets through neighborhoods lined by small houses with old soiled furniture on the porches or in the yards. Old cars on rotted tires, seized by rust, persisting beyond repair or explanation. Old ladies with opaque stockings rolled down to their ankles, searching for reasons to complain. Old men bonded to rocking chairs. Still. Fishermen waiting for someone to take the bait—and stop long enough to listen.

Sometimes, Morton let his thoughts fall away, so he could listen: To the man two seats ahead, complaining to the entire bus how he had just been fined by a "donkey's ass" of a traffic judge. "Seventy two dollars for asking the shit ass police for directions. All the damn' streets blocked off for a Brave's game and construction. Twenty minutes driving around and around…couldn't get my ass out of Atlanta. Saw some cops and drove down to ask for directions. Shit ass of a sergeant woman asked for my licence and insurance instead. Said I was on a street for buses only. Told the shit I was lost…couldn't find my way to the highway. She turn around an' called another shit cop who called me illiterate…said I was old enough to read street signs…asked how I got my licence. Then…gave me a ticket. Five cop cars to give me a ticket. Judge didn't want to hear anything from me. Said it wasn't the job of the police to give directions. Fined me seventy two dollars. Shit, man. Seventy two dollars. Now, I ain't got money for gas. Would like to shit in that judge's face."

"Or in his mouth," another passenger said.

Murmurs of agreement popped up around the bus. Heads nodded. "That's right," from others. A man clapped his hands.

Another voice joined in. A woman of about fifty: "Used to have a small rental house off Cascade Road. Tenant was a woman working in the same office. Two years in the house, and I subsidizing the rent. Said she wanted to buy the place…asked me for a letter for the Mortongage company; then went and bought another house. Trashed my house.

Garbage and stuff everywhere. Carpet black with crud. Nastiest woman I ever saw. Took her to small-claims court. Judge blamed me for everything. Told the woman all the money she could have claimed from me. From me…. After what she done to me, the judge take her side." The woman shook her head. Still not understanding. Forever hurt by the judge's betrayal.

"That's how it is," said another voice from the back. Deep, slow, old. "Courts ain't set up to help poor folk. Law there to protect criminals. If a man mess with you, ain't no use going to the law. Either forget about it…or handle it yourself. Law ain't no use to poor folk. I find a man on my property, and I ain't calling no cops to protect my property. I call them to remove the damn' body."

Law ain't no use to poor folk…. Morton repeated the man's words to himself. Unless the poor folk were like Augustus Telamon who had buried himself so deeply into the law, that it had become a carapace, shielding himself and his activities from legal and political scrutiny.

In the evenings, Judge Telamon hurried home earlier than usual so that he could have a hurried dinner with Dirk, and talk until near midnight. Exchanging ideas for experience. "I had two other friends," the judge said, "superb intellects in economics and medicine. And I was years ahead of my other classmates in law. We could have had comfortable lives, but forever second class. Hard work and excellent qualifications don't always take you where you want to go. Other people would make decisions for us—whether we wanted them to or not. Fact of life. None of us found this tolerable. We got what we wanted. We're exactly where we want to be, now.

"We were eminently practical men. We could not politely ask people to move out of our way. Sometimes our only way through was to remove an obstacle. And we used the most effective means. With sufficient money, there is little one cannot buy in this country…including love. And especially politics. Every politician in this city and this state runs at our pleasure. We give them free reign to wallow in as much garbage as they think they must. But they know their indebtedness. Everyone of them has been bought."

"What was the point?" Morton asked. "You men were wealthy and powerful. What more did you want? And why risk your reputations and your wealth?"

"For…meaning…a rational explanation for our existence," Telamon replied. "Have you ever considered what lies beyond our present lives? What if there is nothing? What if the *'rest is silence,'* as Hamlet said."

And Morton added:

*"The undiscovered country from whose bourn
no traveler returns, puzzles the will,"*

"Exactly. It began as an intellectual challenge. If there was nothing beyond, at least our lives would have changed the course of history. That's what we enjoyed thinking. It became a game, then a habit, then a compulsion. The more we had, the more we wanted…and got.

"But the real reason," said Morton.

"I beg your pardon?" Telamon asked.

"To feel that strongly about acquiring power and influence requires an overwhelming impulse. Something is missing in what you've told me. Something that made you angry beyond endurance…as my parents' murder made me."

Judge Telamon smiled, "Goodness, you don't let anything pass. Do you? Look, we were the first in our families to go to college…and we thought we were special. We expected people to acknowledge our achievements. But we weren't that special, there were thousands like us; maybe not as exceptional, but successful too. That was a little disappointing. But it was the contempt we faced that made the hurt unbearable…the absolute, sneering contempt that we met. In the faces of strangers, shopkeepers, bus drivers. Contempt for us because of what we were, what we looked like…that lumped us with pee-soaked drunks on a park bench…or the losers who had dropped out of everything except begging. We wanted to tell those people that we had done exactly what they kept telling us to do. We had succeeded. We were prepared to apologize for our success if they wanted. Then we discovered as we became more financially secure, that public approval did not matter as much as we had wanted. Even now, our positions do not protect us from discourtesies or insults from some idiot. But how important can that be when you can have that person…fired after a brief 'phone call? Very often, the retribution is great deal more painful than the slight…I assure you. And…although you and I would hesitate to admit it publicly, our daily experiences tell us that most people are stupid. Just drive around the city for fifteen minutes; read the letters to the editor in any newspaper; look at television for an hour; listen to talk radio; listen to our politicians…even the few capable of intelligible speech…. Of course it is not politic to say such things aloud." Telamon's lower lip quivered, as if his anger had brought him near to tears. "What we do, Morton, is control the controllers. It is we who decide who wins a war, wins an election, or…continues to exit."

"And when you…die?" Morton asked.

"There will be others to take our place. You must know that we have not invested so much in you because we love your looks."

"How many others are there?" Morton asked.

"Not yet, Morton," Telamon answered. "Too early for that question…and I am not certain that I could answer it. We are everywhere: In the Congress and in the White House, in every state, the judiciary, universities, in every major business, and in several other countries. We know everything, but seldom interfere…even when it would be to our advantage to do so. Most of our employees or agents do not know the names and faces of more than four others. We deliberately set about to build an entity that was invincible. If one hundred of us were to be killed, the Organization would not miss a step."

"What is my rôle in your organization?"

"That is what we will find out in the next few years. You will show us what you can do. As you asked, we gave you the raw materials. And we are going to invest even more in you. As soon as you feel the ennui coming on, you will be ready. No rush, but there are even more important things to learn in the next few years. We were impressed with you because you understood at a very early age what power meant. At sixteen you knew exactly what it took us most of a lifetime to discover." He leaned forward, and spoke reverently, "We have been searching for years in schools throughout the country for young men like you. You are a very rare person, Morton. I'd say one in several million."

"Thank you, sir."

"Morton? I'd like to ask something of you. I admit it's a matter of vanity, but you have brought such satisfaction into my life for so many years, that I cannot conceive of you as anything but my son. If you called me 'Dad' it would make me very happy."

Augustus Telamon had left out the part of his story that he remembered most clearly, even after almost half a century: The crash of hard footsteps coming to his room—loud, as if the walkers had greater ownership of the house than his parents. The door opening and the man in the doorway taking up the entire rectangle of space. And: "Come."

To his parents' bedroom with his father tied to a chair and his mother lying on her back on the bed, naked, arms and legs spread wide with ropes tied to the bedposts. Both parents trembling so violently that the chair and bed rattled. Refusing to look at him. There was another man sitting on the bed facing his father. He held a revolver in his lap.

Both men wore felt hats pulled low over their brows so that Augustus could not see their faces clearly. The man who had come to his room undressed slowly and climbed over his mother. Morton turned away. The sitting man turned to him. "Look at your mother."

The man lying on his mother did not hurry. When he was done, he dressed carefully then nodded to his companion. The second man raised the revolver and shot his father in the middle of his forehead. Then, turned to the mother and shot her in the temple.

They walked out of the room and out of the house without looking at him. It was almost noon before he managed to escape from the chair, his arms and legs skinned and bleeding. No relative wanted to take him in. The authorities kept him in a roomat a psychiatric hospital until the gray man came to see him. Tall, cadaveric, and gray: skin, hair, eyes, tongue. His voice like gray, weathered wood splintering. "I have asked to adopt you. My name is Telamon."

Augustus Haven was too terrified to refuse. The older Telamon welcomed him into the large, gray, stone house with two libraries. "Yours," he said to the boy.

Telamon remembered well all those things. But he had had more time practicing the story he told to Morton Dirk. "We own large portions of the shares of every major industry and company in the United States and in Western Europe, and enormous tracts of real estate. If the three of us died together, at this moment, some national governments would flounder. Some cities in this country would cease to function. Remember what happened to New York when they went bankrupt? This is where we are. Do we have enough? Enough for what? None of us needs money. None of us wanted a conventional family. I was the only one who married. And regretted it...until my wife died. The reason for our lives is this: power. This, Morton, is the most satisfying possession in existence. Better than fame, better than sex, better than love."

The next morning, at breakfast, Morton said to Judge Telamon, "Time for me to get busy."

And six days after Morton returned from Harvard for the last time, he met his new tutor. Morton was in the library reading when Mr. Mountrie came into the room to call Telamon to the back foyer. He returned with a light-complexioned black man who stood just under six feet, wore a dark brown suit, ecru shirt, brown tie, and brown suede half boots. There was a vagueness about his face as if the contours of his face melded together too gradually for any feature to stand out. Or, as if he stood behind a faint cloud. He looks like me, Morton thought.

Telamon introduced them. "Morton Dirk, Clarence Point."

The men shook hands. "Mr. Point is an expert in…effectiveness. He will teach you the skills you will require."

Point did not react to the introduction. Did not nod or smile.

"When do we start? And where?" Morton asked.

"Here, in the basement," Point said, "tomorrow." He paused, "Do you have a strong stomach, Mr. Dirk?"

"Yes," Morton said.

"Eight o'clock tomorrow morning." He turned to the judge, "Do you need me for anything else, sir?"

Augustus Telamon accompanied the brown man out of the library. When he came back, he was serious. "I don't have to tell you what Point is going to teach you. He's the best in his field of expertise. He's about the only man who makes me nervous. Now, I shall have two men to fear." He smiled, but Morton did not see any fear in his eyes.

And no smile on Clarence Point's face the following morning—if that were his name, Morton thought. No expression, no interest, as if he were asleep with his eyes open. Totally self-controlled—like the man who had ordered the deaths of his parents. Morton stared at Point's face trying to remember some peculiarity. Nothing. He could not remember his tutor's face a few seconds after looking away.

"You remind me of a man I met about seven years ago," Morton said.

"Don't think so," the other man said.

"Same vague face…" Morton said.

He might as well have spoken to a rock. Point ignored the comment.

"Judge Telamon told me you are a black belt in karate. I would like to measure your skill…in your street clothes," Point said. His left leg was already lancing toward Morton's face before he had finished speaking.

Morton dove to the right, but not before the edge of Point's heel grazed his left cheekbone, burning the skin as if a lighted match had touched it. He felt a brief panic—the first time since he witnessed his parents' death; then he was cold again; and angry. He hit the floor rolling quickly to the left, and exploded upwards, his right heel aimed at Point's right temple. He hit air, and the back of his head exploded. He fell to his knees and shook his head and threw himself forward. Heard the whip of Point's feet, rolled on his back and kicked out blindly. Both legs. Hard. Felt the shock of Point's shoe against his. He rolled to the right fast, and was up on his feet again. He was smiling. Point was coming again, fast, but the smile had slightly disturbed his composure—he hesitated just long enough for Morton to read his move. He was still too fast. Morton leaped to the right, balanced on the ball of his right foot and kicked out with his left foot at Point's airborne body. Morton felt his heel nick Point's left shoulder, but the man was already rolling to the right, away from the kick. He landed on his feet, stumbled, but before Morton could move in, Point had kicked his legs out from under him. Point was as good as Saul Yura, his old teacher in Boston. Morton steeled his body for the blinding pain, but nothing happened. The noises in the room came from his heart and lungs. He glanced at his watch: less than ten minutes had passed since he had entered the basement.

Point stood six feet away breathing calmly. "This is good enough for public demonstration. What I am going to teach you in the next two months is how to kill an experienced black-belt. We start tomorrow morning. I am not teaching you how to counter an opponent, or how to hurt him. I am teaching you how to kill him...and quickly. No survivable injury or pain to your opponent. You understand me?"

"Yes."

"We practice three hours every morning, and three every afternoon. Every other day for a week, then every day for another week. First week easier, so your body can adjust. Two months. Then we move on to weapons."

"Yes."

Point headed for the doorway. His clothes damp and torn. One of his eyes was swollen.

Morton's upper lip and his left cheek were was cut and bleeding; both palms were skinned. The rest of his body felt as if he had been beaten with a baseball bat for an hour. His clothes were ruined, and shoes badly scuffed.

"Who trained you?" Morton asked, as Point went out the door.

"U. S. Government," Point answered.

"SEALS? Marines?"

But Point was halfway up the stairs. He did not answer or turn around.

That was the first day of two months of agony and bruising; and one broken small toe for Morton Dirk. When it was over, he discovered that he could lower his heart rate at will; and could reduce the blood flow to his extremities, shunting more of it to his brain until his senses were so acute that he could almost anticipate Point's moves. Until he could force his instructor into defending himself. He knew he was changing too, becoming more like Point: cold and unfeeling; having to make an effort to be pleasant with the house staff; exchanging smiles for Mrs. Mountrie's occasional pleasantries because he wanted to improve his cooking skills—while he considered which of her kitchen knives would sever a neck; perhaps her neck. He imagined floating up quietly behind her while she spoke, and slicing through her neck so swiftly that the words would continue to come through the gash in her throat before she collapsed, her eyes wide with incomprehension. Death coming before she could feel the pain.

He did not like guns. Point did not either: too much noise; too heavy and conspicuous; too many traces like powder burns; groove markings on slugs and casings; difficult to carry on a plane. "But people are going to point guns at you; and you may have to use one yourself. Better learn how to use one."

Point went to a large suitcase in a corner of the basement, and lifted it onto a table. The weight made him grunt. "Got ten handguns in here, and a couple of submachine guns. Pick them up one at a time; handle them for a while; point them at something; feel them for weight."

Morton handled the guns for ten minutes. Picked up an automatic with a dull black plastic finish. "Like this one," he said.

Point's face remained impassive. "Yours. It's been tested. Works well."

"Good gun?" Dirk asked.

"All good guns. You're the one who's got to be good. I'll take you to a private firing range this afternoon. Two months on guns. You've got to be able to hit a man's eye at fifty feet...the one I will tell you to hit. Now, I want you to take the gun apart and put it back again. Watch me do it first." He took the gun from Morton, began to disassemble it.

After lunch, they drove to an isolated farm house in Cherokee County. Three miles from the highway along a dirt road through pine and oaks. "We'll be here one week," he said at the door. "Coming back tomorrow, so pack some clothes tonight."

An old white lady with no make-up other than a splash of scarlet lipstick, opened the door. "Balott's down in the basement. Go on down." She moved back to let them in; showed no interest in either of them; did not wait for introductions.

Morton followed Point down into the basement. The woman closed the door at the top of the stairs. A brightly lit room hung with quilted padding. Human outlines and paper bull's-eyes on targets stood at the long end of the room. Point nodded at a barrel-chested man with a thin beard but no mustache. Jeans and blue denim shirt mottled with oil and grease; wrinkles in his hands and face traced with black. "Morton Dirk," Point said.

The man looked at Morton: no smile, eyes gray and cold. The eyes moved down his body, back up again. "Balott." he said, accentuation on the second syllable.

"Yes," Morton said.

Point opened a brief case. Two pistols nestled in black foam inserts. Handed Morton the pistol he had chosen. "Glock...ten millimeter," he said to Balott.

Balott took down black ear protectors and eye shields from hooks on a wall. Handed Point and Morton one of each. "I'll go first," he said. Lifted a long barreled stainless steel revolver from a table. The small frown on his face disappeared as he lifted the revolver toward the target. "First man on left. Right eye...then heart." There was a hint of elation in his voice.

The gun exploded six times in three seconds. Their eyes still seeing orange blades of flame from the gun barrel when Balott put down the Smith and Wesson magnum. The target was swaying but the right eye had become a large irregular hole and there was another hole just left of center of the chest. "Ain't missed in five years," Balott said to the target. His lips were drawn back in a tight grimace to show surprisingly good teeth.

Perhaps he was smiling, Morton thought. He breathed in the smoke. Enjoyed the smell. It reminded him of fireworks on the Fourth of July.

Balott turned to him. "Load your gun. Left eye's yours. Six shots," he said.

Morton hit the head once, and the chest twice, and the right elbow once. Missed with the other two shots.

"Good," Balott said.

"Good?" Morton asked. Waited for an explanation.

"You would have killed him, anyway."

"But I didn't hit the left eye," Morton said.

"How many times you done this before?" Balott asked.

"First time."

"Then, good." And Balott picked up a new target and went to replace the one they had shot through.

Morton glanced at Point. Still no sign of life. Or interest, as Point lifted the other pistol from its nest in the briefcase. He aimed casually at the new target as if he were bored. One second of thunder, and the left eye of the target had disappeared.

Balott said to Morton: "Point the gun at the target. Support your right hand and gun with your left hand. Gun at arm's length. Slow down your heart. Hold your breath. Look at your target. Follow the bullet to its hit. Nothing else in your mind...but satisfaction. Keep rehearsing that in your mind. We'll try again tomorrow. Try again." Morton did no better.

"We have to leave now," Point said after Morton's second attempt. His words like gunshots. He looked toward their host. "Balott," he said and went up the stairs.

After six weeks, Morton thought he was good enough to challenge Balott or Point, but thought better of it. They would probably have ignored him.

But he was good with a knife. He has seen the faint flicker of Point's eyebrows when he sliced through a watermelon without disturbing the fruit sitting in the other's outstretched hands. He preferred thin blades, single-edged, honed until they could shave the hair on the back of his hand.

"Buy kitchen knives...good enough for one job. And discard them afterwards." Point said.

One evening, after a workout, Point said: "Tomorrow's your last day in training, but I have to keep you ready, so I'll be seeing you occasionally. Couple of other little things." He took a black vial out of his jacket pocket. "Poison tablets...quick and effective. Keep them out of the light and heat. Only two tablets in the bottle. If you need more, you will get them. Don't touch them unless you're wearing gloves. They're strong enough to kill if you hold them in your hand for fifteen seconds...five seconds if your hands are sweating. No antidote that I know of." He reached into his jacket again and took out a nine-inch black-handled knife in a black leather sheath. Pulled it out. The blade was almost as thin as paper. "Careful not to bend it, blade's brittle but sharper than a scalpel. If you cut yourself with this, you won't feel a thing...but you'd probably bleed to death. For practice," he said.

"Thanks," Morton said. It was a gift, but he did not expect Point to say so.

After the last training session, Point carted his collection of carrying cases from the basement. He did not ask for help, but Morton helped him carry them to a black van.

Point said, "Next Wednesday evening, I have a problem to solve. Judge Telamon wants you to come along. Dress very casually in grey or brown. No cologne or scents on you...shower with Ivory soap...use unscented deodorant. No identification, not even cash." He drove away.

That night, at dinner, Telamon ate quickly, anxious to relay the good news. But he waited until Morton had finished. "Point says you're good."

"In theory," Morton answered.

"Chance for some experience on Wednesday evening."

"May I ask what the problem is?" Morton asked.

"An impediment in Marietta." Judge Telamon said, "Point will fill you in. Best not to know too much too early."

"I understand. My application to Charteris was accepted. I start teaching in the Fall."

"Good, good, good. Should be very busy with all you've got to do. Think you can handle it?" Telamon asked.

"I'm enjoying myself. Don't see any problem. Another thing: About time I found a place of my own. Can't keep smooching off you," Morton said.

"Think it over a bit. You've been good company for me. But...if you change your mind, it would make me happy."

"Yes...yes of course." It would be difficult calling the judge "Dad." Too sentimental, almost maudlin. Telamon must be sensing his mortality.

Morton did not think about the mission again until Wednesday evening when Point drove to the house in a dirty and faded gray Chevrolet Citation. He was wearing a brown jacket over a black shirt and black slacks. He looked Morton over. "Good." Handed him a pair of black latex gloves. "Put them on before you touch the car, and keep them on until you get back here. It you're too nervous, they'll fill with sweat."

"I understand," Morton said.

Before they left, exactly at ten, he removed the van's rear licence plate and replaced it with another he took from a brown padded envelope. "Let's go," he said to Morton.

Neither spoke until they were on Highway 75 North. "I do all the talking. No questions or action from you…not even if things get tricky. Just fade into the background. Look and listen to everything. Every situation will be different, and you will have to improvise, but the principle is the same: you remain in control…total control…all the time. Once you have started you must complete the job. Never consider a change of mind. What you body does is secondary to what your mind does. Absolute focus and remain calm. Absolute focus on your first weapon: your voice. The knife, or whatever you choose is for completion. You understand me?"

"Perfectly," Morton answered. Leaned back and let his body relax. His breathing slowed and hands became cooler. He asked again: "Who is the 'impediment?'"

"All the information we work with comes on a diskette; sometimes Judge Telamon passes it on. Sometimes, another person in the Organization. I have a software program that decodes it.

Gives you everything you need to know about the situation. Description, habits…good and bad…even what they scream in bed. Until you feel like the target's soul mate. How to get close enough for the job , and how to get out again. Every piece of shit you need to know. I don't know how the Organization gets all this stuff. Stopped even wondering what they know about me. Probably know how you fold the toilet paper to wipe your butt."

"What do you know about this person we're going to see?"

"Looks like a partner in a firm important to the Organization has been collecting confidential information over the past six months. He goes into the office at night, between eleven and one, to access data and correspondence files. We believe he will take these to the Attorney General."

"How did you find out when he returns to the office?" Morton asked.

"The cleaning staff—they're highly valued employees."

"And he's busy right now?" Morton asked.

"Must be, he came in at nine tonight. Must have a lot to do…wrapping up, probably. How is your stomach?" Point asked.

"Fine. More anticipation than apprehension. I told you I have a strong stomach."

"We'll see."

They pulled into the parking lot of an office complex on Cobb Parkway. "Black building up ahead, eleventh floor. We take the elevator to the ninth…walk up the rest," Point said.

They parked behind the building, and walked to a back door. Point pulled out a key. "Alarm's been turned off. Security will stay at the front until twelve. We take the service elevator."

On the ninth floor, Morton followed Point to the emergency exit door, and up the stairs to the eleventh floor. The hallway was dark except for the red exit signs. Point walked to the glass doors of an office numbered 1106. Unlocked them slowly, stopped in the middle of the reception area, and stood still, listening carefully for several seconds. They turned left, down another hallway, past two doors. Stopped at the third door on the left. There was a flickering sliver of light under the door, and the sound of rapid tapping on a computer keyboard. Point inserted another key and turned slowly. It seemed an entire minute to Morton. Point pressed down on the handle of the door and opened gently. No sound—the cleaners had oiled the hinges and the lock. The door opened wider and Morton could see the profile of the man sitting at a computer. The man saw them at almost the same moment and lunged for the desk drawer.

"No."

The hand stopped inches away from the desk; and the man looked into the aperture of the silencer on a heavy black automatic—clear, even in the dim light. He sat back and placed both hands on the writing pad on the desk, palms down.

Point walked to the desk and turned the fluorescent lamp on.

The face was younger than Morton had expected. Thin, very dark skinned. Eyes framed by gold-rimmed glasses, hair cut close to the scalp. Still dressed for work in a pinstriped navy blue suit. About thirty year's old. His sharp handsome face at first frozen in terror then relaxing slightly as if relieved by the acknowledgment of a conclusion to his actions. His eyes went quickly about the office—remembering the last things he would see.

"Where are the previous files?" Point asked.

The man's eyes indicated a grey plastic file carrier. "Previous diskettes?"

The man forced his mouth open, licked his lips. Rasped. "Everything's here."

"You understand that in a short while, you will be dead. You knew that was a possibility when you began your quest. You do not have a choice in the consequences. What I shall offer you is a choice in the manner in which you will die. If you force me to kill you, I shall also kill your wife and two children. If you do it yourself, I shall spare your family, and they will be taken care of financially. Modestly, of course. Our problem is with you, not with your family."

The voice was warm and comforting, soothing even Morton's tension—making him feel that he was watching a staged drama.

The man's face relaxed completely, his eyes widening as if waiting to express his thankfulness.

"Are there any more files? I am asking for the last time," Point said again.

The man reached into his jacket.

"Stop." Point's voice was like a hammer blow to the head.

The man froze.

"Open your jacket with your left hand…slowly. Okay, two fingers…right hand into your pocket…slowly. Put the diskette on the desk. Good. Is that all?"

"Yes. All." the man said.

"Take your gun out of the drawer…slowly. Put the barrel to your right temple. Bring your hand down a bit. Angle the gun upwards. Stop. Goodbye Mr. Trestall. Your wife will receive a letter from you and an envelope containing two hundred and fifty thousand dollars within the week. That is all. Please pull the trigger."

The noise deafened them. The reverberations continued as Point picked up the files. He inserted a diskette taken from his pocket into the computer and accessed the drive. The information on the screen changed as the hard drive was destroyed. He retrieved the diskette. They walked out of the office, their ears still ringing. In the elevator, Point asked again: "How's your stomach?"

"Noise made it contract. Louder than I had expected. Probably because I had worn ear protectors before."

"That's why I don't like guns. Crude."

"Phalluses for punks," Morton said.

"And red necks,"

No one saw them leave the building. No one took any notice of the old gray vehicle leaving the parking lot.

"When I was a kid," Point said as they drove south on the highway, "it was so much easier to see the stars. Now, with all the city lights, all you can see sometimes is the Orion constellation. December is a good month for stars."

"A long time ago," Morton said, "I tried to impress a girl by pointing out Ursa Major and the North Star. Never tried that crap again. Whole school knew about it the next day. Called me 'Star Boy' for weeks."

Point was sympathetic. "Kids are so damn' wicked."

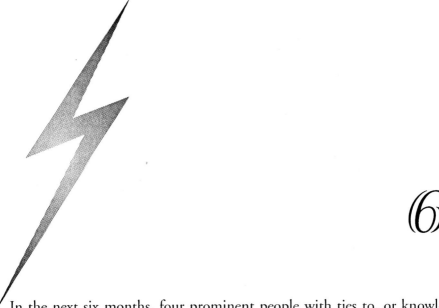

6

In the next six months, four prominent people with ties to, or knowledge of Judge August Telamon's organization died: A public prosecutor in Miami, Florida; the chairman of a small aircraft manufacturing company in Seattle, Washington; the owner of one of Idaho's largest agribusinesses; and the chairwoman of a New York investment firm. Those deaths were mentioned in the city newspapers, but no connection was made between the deaths. Their causes were all different: an auto accident, electrocution, drowning, and poisoning. All accidental. The papers did not mention the death of a private investigator in Minneapolis, Minnesota, because he was not a prominent citizen; and because his connection to the other four victims was not known to anyone other than the three men who called themselves Augustus, Hadrian and Galba.

Morton Dirk received twenty five thousand dollars for his presence at each of the five deaths; and instructions for depositing most of that money in an offshore bank account in the Caribbean. After his third mission, he used some of it for the down payment on a two-bedroom brick cottage in a quiet residential area in east of Atlanta. Mostly retirees; few newcomers and children. Not much grass to mow; flower beds at the front; a vegetable garden in the fenced back yard and a trellis with mature grape vines along the north fence. He bought a used Ford van. Dark brown, nondescript. The telephone company installed one telephone with an unlisted number. Clarence Point came with another a man to install another telephone. That one had no number. The man also installed a computer.

There were no introductions, and he did not acknowledge Morton's presence. When he was done, and ensured that the computer was working, Point selected the program menu and highlighted a file named JOURNEY. "This will read the information on the diskettes you will get from the Organization. You will be able to read it only once. And the information cannot be saved. The menu is similar to Windows. Choose a five-digit password, preferably alphanumeric. Do not record it anywhere. Okay, enter it here. Good. You're on your own now."

There were no more assignments for the remainder of the year, and Morton did not see Point during that time. He prepared for his classes.

His first lecture at Charteris University was in September, on a Tuesday morning still warm enough for T-shirts, shorts and shorter skirts. Warm classrooms, restless bodies. Twenty faces looked back at him with disinterest, nonchalance, or mild curiosity. Most in their early twenties; some with wedding bands; three with occasional strands of gray. Not what the women had hoped for: He was well-dressed, but so...ordinary. And the men had expected someone older...or more professorial. But his voice startled them: It came like a hand that reached out and grabbed each by the throat and said: It does not matter what you think of me...but you will listen.

He said: "My job is to reintroduce you with humanity's greatest triumph— language. The probability that you understand what I am saying means that you use language. And your presence here indicates your intent to use it more effectively. Most of you wish to be writers. At the end of this course, you will know with all certainty whether that wish should be pursued. This morning's lecture will be on poetry: the most common, most beautiful, most difficult, and the most abused of the language arts. Let me tell you what good poetry is not: it is not the assembly of lines so that the last words rhyme. Good poetry is the use of language to paint pictures in the mind. Good poetry elicits envy. It must make the listener wonder: How did the poet do that? How did he find those words? The good poet does not take careful steps. He or she leaps magnificently from image to image…so wonderfully, that the listener is left breathless, unable to savor one image before another, even more fantastic, arrives. Good poetry is not casual, it is not private. It is also dangerous. It bares the writer's soul to scrutiny. To write a good poem is to open one's life to public view. It is not the ten minutes of scribbling of indecipherable assemblages of word on a bit of paper. In short, ladies and gentlemen, poetry is serious business. For the rest of the morning, I shall give you some examples of how the great poets have expressed very ordinary emotions: love, vice, humor, and even eroticism. Good stuff. Listen to the fearless magnificent sounds. Examine the pictures that leap across your mind. Open your ears."

Twenty pairs of eyes were locked on face, afraid to leave it even for movements beyond the windows of the room: five ravens convening on the branches of a poplar; two students sharing the weight of a backpack; cars entering and leaving the parking garage at the end of the green; movements accompanying unheard conversations.

"I shall start with love. From two poets writing in the language of love. Senghor of Senegal; and Baudelaire of France. One an African, and the other a white Frenchman in love with a black Haitian woman. First, Léopold Senghor's *Femme Noire*, Black woman:

Naked woman, dark woman
Ripe fruit with firm flesh, somber ecstasies of black wine, mouth
making my mouth lyrical.

"Listen again, think of the words: fruit, wine, lyrical. Would you have used these in a love poem? Simple words evoking taste, texture, intoxication and words…more words.

"And from Monsieur Beaudelaire's *A Hemisphere in a Woman's Hair*. Remember, these are translations from the original French, and so suffer a loss in the sounds of the words:

> *'Let me breathe for a long, long time, the perfume of your hair, and plunge my face into it, like a thirsty man in the water of a spring, and shake it in my hand like a scented handkerchief, so that I might wave memories in the air.'*

"This last was written for Jeanne Duval, a mulatto woman who inspired his best work, and who it is said also caused his greatest miseries.

"Next, let us look at how the Persian poet speaks of drunkenness in the Rubaiyat of Omar Khayyam, in the version by Edward Fitzgerald:

> *'Oh my Belovèd, fill the Cup that clears*
> *To-day of past Regrets and future*
> *Fears—*
> *Tomorrow?—Why, To-morrow I may*
> *be*
> *Myself with Yesterday's Sev'n Thousand*
> *Years.'*

"And even more delightfully:

> *'You know, my Friends, how long since*
> *in my House*
> *For a new Marriage I did make*
> *Carouse:*
> *Divorced old barren Reason from my*
> *Bed,*
> *And took the Daughter of the Vine to*
> *Spouse.'*

"And while you're smiling, consider this mischievous look at religious intolerance from An Oriental Apologue, by James Russell Lowell:

'Each from his hut rushed six score times a day,
Like a great canon of the Church full-rammed
With cartridge theologic (so to say,)
Touched himself off, and then, recoiling, slammed
His hovel's door behind him in a way
That to his foe said plainly,— you'll be damned;'

"And while we're touching a religious theme, consider the dilemma of Francis Thompson in *The Hound of Heaven*, where he hesitates to give himself up to his faith because he must then abjure worldly pleasures:

'(For, though I knew His love Who followèd,
Yet was I sore adread
Lest, having Him, I must have naught beside).'

"Can you appreciate the poet's dilemma? We've all experienced it: I want to be good, but not yet. Just a little more fun…just this one time. And you can see the effect this uncertainty has had on some religious faiths, where pleasure is considered a temptation to sin, or even sinful in itself.

"Finally, what you have all been waiting for: eroticism. And from an unexpected source, the Uraguyan poet, Delmira Agustini, writing at the turn of the century. This is from her *Otra estirpe*, Another Race.

'The electric corolla that I unfold today
yields the nectar of a garden of Wives;
in my flesh I deliver up to his vultures
a whole swarm of pink doves.'

"Amazed? And there is more:"

'Lying here in this way, I am an ardent furrow
where the seed of another sublimely mad race
can be nourished!'"

"Oh, my God, she's talking about a woman's…a woman's…." Millie Vance looked around the class for support.

"A woman's what?" Professor Dirk asked.

"A woman's…private stuff…you know?" Millie said.

All their eyes were on his face, wanting his own words for what they already knew, because he could say it better—with less prurience.

"Yes, Ms. Vance," Dirk said, "It's a woman's most private and precious gift to her lover. It's the poet's bouquet of flowers, with all its colors, scents and nectars. It is exactly what you think she is saying. Only, she has said it more boldly and beautifully than most of us could have.…Which is what good poetry is. Which is why her poetry still exists. Tragically, Almira Agustini was killed by her husband after a very brief marriage because, some say, of her love for another man, the Argentinian poet, Manuel Ugarte."

"Holy shit." Most of the class heard Timothy Russell's whisper.

"Yes, there is nothing subtle about this piece. And when you have regained some measure of composure, I would like you to explore for yourselves the way some poets—of your choosing, have dealt with life's common themes: death, war, uncertainty, or whatever. At least three examples from each person; and please be prepared to tell us why each piece has moved you. It does not matter if several of you choose the same work. We shall go over these in one week today. I shall see you in two days."

Later that night, or tomorrow night, he would drive to Judge Augustus Telamon's estate to repeat some of the lecture. In past recitations in the library, the judge had sat in a cordovan leather recliner with his eyes shut, careful that his stirring or breathing did not disturb the speaker. Sometimes, he dabbed at small sparkling crescents below his closed eyelids. Yes, Dad would be anxious to know how his first class had gone. He would probably call Mr. Peter Hall and Mr. Charles John to tell them more about the wonder he had discovered.

The fall semester ended. Professor Dirk was beyond adequate praise, his students said. Two of the women who sat in the front row of his class gave up trying to draw his eyes to their bared thighs. And he was not that attractive, anyway.

He wiped his notes off the chalkboard and turned around to take his notes off the desk when he noticed Millie Vance still at her seat. Her face tight with fear; her right thumb tapping incessantly against the index finger.

"I need to talk to you," she said.

His mind raced, trying to find anything that could connect his actions to the student. Nothing.

"My office…or here? he asked.

"Office." The word was a struggle.

He turned to the door and was in his office for five minutes before she knocked on the door.

He pulled a chair for her to the front of the desk. Sat and waited. Let his breathing slow.

She looked around the room, at everything but him. Stared suddenly at his hands clasped on the writing tablet. "I'm pregnant."

He frowned. "Should you be telling me this, Ms. Vance?"

"I need…I need…. I cant' go through with it."

"But why me?"

"Don't know anybody else I can ask."

"Ask what?" Dirk asked.

"I can't go alone. I want somebody to come with me."

He relaxed slightly. Her situation had nothing to do with him. "Are you going to have an abortion?" he asked.

She nodded.

"And you want me to come with you?"

She looked back at him open-mouthed. Her silence pleading.

"When?" he asked.

"I have an appointment at three, day after tomorrow."

"Anybody else know about this?" he asked.

"The father knows I'm pregnant, but not what I'm going to do."

"And he would object?"

"Yes."

"Not surprised. Tran Duc struck me as an honorable man," Morton said.

Millie eyes widened. She almost screamed at him. "How did you know?"

"I'm at the front of the class. I can see all faces. Who looks at whom…and how. Things you couldn't see. Tran has not been able to keep his eyes off you for the past week. And he has been distracted. I can tell from his work."

"Oh, Lord," Millie Vance said. "Are you going to…?"

"Tell? No, that's not my business. So, how can I help?"

"I need somebody to take me home afterwards. I might not be able to drive."

"Want me to take you there?"

"Well, I didn't want you to get embarrassed. They may think you're the father."

"Don't worry about that. I'll take you there…and wait. You'll be fine."

Two days later, he drove to the airport, left his car in the airport parking lot and walked through the baggage claim to the car-rental agencies. Rented a black Cavalier. Then he drove to her address. She was waiting. Got into his car quickly.

"How are you?" he asked.

"Scared. Really, really scared."

He walked with her into the clinic. Waited while she signed some forms, then was taken into another room. A lady came back out five minutes later, and crooked her finger at him. She was plump, and her face creased quickly into the tiny smiles of practiced reassurance. "She'll be ready to go home in two hours."

"Thanks."

He drove to the county library, and sat at the magazine rack reading until four-thirty. He was back at the clinic at ten minutes before five.

The smiling lady came out to the waiting room. "She's waiting. She's doing okay. Thinks she can walk to the car, but we'll get her out on a chair. I'll go get her. If you'll drive to the side." She pointed to her left.

Another woman wheeled Millie Vance into the waiting room. "I'll give you a quick ride to the car, darling."

"No," Millie said. "I can walk." She refused Morton's arm. Did not look at his face.

The attendant placed an arm on her shoulder. "Got to give you a ride to the car, honey."

He followed them to the car.

Millie's hands trembled so violently that he had to help her with the seat belt. As he walked around to the driver's side, the clinic attendant asked: "You'll be okay?"

He was about to say that he was not responsible for Millie's pregnancy, but that would be to abandon her. Too callous. And he was enjoying the novel role of protector. "She's the tough one," he said. The woman smiled her approval.

It was dark when they arrived at her apartment. She handed him her keys.

She walked slowly and stiffly to the door. He let them in. The apartment was spotless as if to welcome guests. "What can I get you? Water?" he asked.

"Please," she said. She drank three glasses of water.

"How do you feel?" he asked.

"Cramps," she said. "I need to lie down."

She stood and this time took his hand. He lifted her on to the bed, took off her shoes. She sat up and began undoing the top buttons of her dress. He finished for her then helped her out of the dress and shift. "Where's your night dress?" he asked.

"Bathroom...behind the door," she said.

He helped her change. "Want me to get you something to eat?"

"Not yet," she said and climbed into the bed. Turned on her side away from him. He sat on a chair near the door. Silent for the next hour. Then she turned toward him. "I'm so sorry, Dr. Dirk, for getting you into this. But I didn't know whom to ask."

"I'm glad you asked me," he said. "This is not the sort of thing a person should handle alone."

"Are you disappointed in me?" she asked.

"I don't make value judgements about people. I've never met a saint. And don't worry about what I think. I look forward to seeing you your usual perky self in class next January."

"I'm glad I asked you…this is a heavy thing to put on somebody…if you had said no, I would have gone alone. Dr. Dirk, I don't want to keep you here any longer. If you have to go…."

Morton rose from the chair and looked at her face. "I don't have to, I can stay the night…if you like. I'll sleep in the living room…on the couch."

She smiled for the first time that day. Nodded.

He was still wide awake almost two hours later when he heard her walk into the living room. She walked slowly to the couch. He sat up. "Something wrong?"

"I want you to come in the bedroom. I'm so scared."

He followed her back. "I'll sit in the chair," he said.

He saw her shake her head in the dim light. She climbed into the bed, and he followed. Lay on his side facing her back.

She pushed herself back into the curve of his body. He rested his cheek lightly against the back of her head, and his voice was so quiet that the words sounded like sheets of paper falling to the ground; or the frisson of trees in the wind.

She tried to hear the actual words, but couldn't find the strength even to listen. Then she was falling. A brief panic. Then she felt him against her, and was calm again.

Five minutes later he heard her breathing slow, then she began snoring.

The next morning, she did not wake when he rose to make breakfast. Cooked her oatmeal in milk, and topped that with slices of a banana and an orange. He noticed that she had stocked her refrigerator well; probably expected to be homebound for some time.

At noon, he prepared to leave.

"I owe you a lot." Millie Vance said.

"No, you don't. Don't even think about it," he said. "Do you think you can manage on you own now?"

"I'll be okay," she said, "already feeling much better."

"How do you think Mr. Duc is going to take the news?"

"When he thinks of the alternative, he'll understand. You know, he actually wanted to get married. Told him that situation would be even worse than the first." She hesitated a moment, then asked: "Want to know how we got involved?"

"No. It's not at all my business." He knew she wanted to talk; to convince him that her action had not made her a bad person; to ensure that she did not need his pity. And if he told her that he did not care, she would think him callous. But her situation was unimportant to him—too many other things to occupy his time. He wanted her to be comfortable and to heal. That was all. And if she could read his mind, know what his best skill was, know that he could kill her with indifference and forget it a minute later?

She tried to smile. "Yeah, guess you're right. Same thing happens to other people all the time. Right?"

"Yes. And worse. How are you for essentials…and money?"

"I'll be okay, now. Thanks. Thank you very much, Dr. Dirk."

"I'll check on you later. If you need me, call my office and leave a message. I'll be away from home for a couple of days, but I'll check for messages…just remembered, I don't have your number."

She wrote it for him on a tissue.

He was at the airport at forty-five minutes later.

Morton spent most of the Christmas vacations in the school library. A dark shape in a cubicle behind the shelves. No one bothered looking twice. All assignments were reviewed in the first two days. Nothing left to do before Christmas but search for more material for classes. A hundred novels to read again; this time quickly.

Dirk telephoned Millie Vance every other day, and visited her twice, before she left to spend Christmas with her parents in Florida. That solved one problem: he had considered asking whether he could spend Christmas day with her. Had wondered what to buy her as a gift.

After his own Christmas dinner with Judge Telamon and some of the household—the maid and gardener had gone to spend the holiday with their families—Telamon handed Morton a black plastic diskette holder. "Something you asked for."

That night, Morton slept in his old bed. The room was exactly as he had left it. Eight years ago.

He turned on the computer as soon as he arrived home. After he entered his password, the screen turned black then white. In the middle in large black upper case letters, it said: Gabriel "Archangel" Caraglo. There were six pages of terse sentences under brief headings: Address, name, age, sex, height, weight, race, hair color, eye color, distinctive marks; and details of Caraglo's habits, affiliations, connections, affairs; and details of his family and friends. Morton spent two hours reading the information. When he exited the program and tried to access the drive again, he received a message warning of an unformatted diskette in the A drive.

On the night of January fifth, at nine o'clock in the evening, he drove to Jonesboro, south of Atlanta, to the collection of warehouses behind the large sign that read Caraglo Imports. He had learned in his previous visits where Caraglo's office was, how many other people worked past five o'clock, where Caraglo parked his car, and what time he left. He also knew that there were two armed guards in the main building, and that they were not garrulous men. Morton drove to a pay telephone a quarter of a mile away. Dialed.

Caraglo's voice said, "Yeah."

"Mr. Caraglo, I am a waiter at Pemmer's Bar and Grill. Somebody left a file on a table with information that I don't think you would want our customers to read."

"What the hell you talking about? What file? What somebody?"

"Okay, it may be another Caraglo, but it says 'Caraglo Imports and it has an address in Jonesboro. And it has a list of names of people in Customs and Immigration, and names of airlines and officials with amounts they received...."

"Hey! Where did you get that shit? You trying to blackmail me or something?"

"Look man, I found a brown folder with a set of papers with people's names and a bunch of stuff about payments. I don't need any hassle or shit from you, man. I can give you your stuff if you pay me for my time. Or I take the shit to the police." Morton's voice was rising.

"Look, okay, let's cool it. I don't know what you got...or if it's mine. Okay? Let me have a look. If it's anything to do with me, I'll pay you, okay?"

The tone of Morton's voice deepened, but remained suspicious. "How much? And how do I know you won't have my ass shot, and you take your papers?"

"And how do I know you ain't trying to rip me off?" Caraglo asked.

"Listen, Caraglo, I'm getting tired of this shit. You want your papers or not?"

"All right, I want to see the papers. If they have anything to do with me, I'll pay you five hundred. If not, two hundred."

"Seven hundred, if they're yours. Three hundred if not. That's it."

"Bring the papers to my office. Know where I am?...Yeah, that's it. How long it'll take you to get here?"

"Thirty, forty minutes," Morton said.

In his office, Caraglo pounded on his desk. "Shit, shit, shit, goddam shit. Who's the shithead who got dropped this stuff." He reached for the telephone, began dialing the home number of Herm Morille, his attorney. Put the handset down after the sixth digit. The fewer people who knew the better. He went to the front desk. "Frankie, there's some guy coming by to bring me a package. Bring him to the office as soon as he comes. Hear?"

"Yeah, boss. What's he look like?" the guard asked.

"Some kind of messenger, how'd I know?"

Forty five minutes later, Frankie's voice came over the desk intercom. "Messenger here with a package, Mr. Caraglo."

"Okay, bring him over."

Caraglo's door was open. The men walked in.

"Okay, Frankie. It's all right. Get back to the front."

The guard hesitated, but the nondescript black man looked harmless...and he wasn't carrying a gun.

"Let's see what you got." Caraglo reached for the padded brown envelope.

"Envelope's empty, Mr. Caraglo," the voice said.

"What the f...." Caraglo began, and reached for the intercom button.

The hand that stopped his felt like pliers. He sat back immediately. He wanted desperately to go to the toilet. He wanted to breathe again. "Who are you? What's going on?" He just managed the words.

"My name's Morton Dirk. My parents worked for you. They were both killed in a hit eight years ago. Why did you kill my parents Mr. Caraglo?"

There was a sudden stink in the room as Caraglo soiled himself. But the terror in his eyes faded slightly as if the man on the other side of the desk had given him an opportunity to vindicate himself.

Then the intercom clicked. "Everything okay in there, boss?" "Yeah, we're talking," Caraglo answered.

"Just checking."

"Thanks, Frankie," Caraglo said.

"Listen, Mr. Dirk, from the bottom of my heart, I didn't kill your parents. I couldn't kill anybody, Mr. Dirk…not even if they had stolen every cent I have. I've had a couple of people beaten up for stealing from the business, but nothing too serious. Just so they won't do it again…to anybody. But kill? No, no, no. I can't have that on my conscience. I have a family, Mr. Dirk."

"Mr. Caraglo, I was in the room when my parents were killed. I heard one man say he had come to collect the money they had stolen from Caraglo. I was there," Morton said.

"I swear to you, Mr. Dirk, I did not kill your parents. I was accused of their murder. The court found me not guilty, Mr. Dirk…."

"Insufficient evidence," Dirk said.

"Because I was the only suspect in the murders, Mr. Dirk." Caraglo said, "but I didn't send anybody after your parents. Let me tell you something Mr. Dirk, this business has my name all over it…but's it's not mine. I only run it. Why should I kill two people for stealing somebody else's money?"

"Whose money, Mr. Caraglo?" Dirk asked.

"I can't tell you that, Mr. Dirk."

"Mr. Caraglo," Morton said, removing a thin-bladed knife from a sheath under the long sleeve of his shirt, "I will count up to two. After that I will kill you. And you know that I will kill you. One…."

"Please."

"Two," and Dirk moved toward Archangel Caraglo.

Caraglo tried to move, tried to force his hand to the intercom button. Could not. His jaw hurt as he forced his mouth open. "Judge…Telamon," he managed to say.

Morton stopped. Found his legs paralyzed. He inhaled hard. His heartbeats were deafening him. "Augustus Telamon?" he whispered through the burning constriction of his throat.

Caraglo nodded quickly. Relaxing slightly again. The two men sat down, their eyes locked. Morton reached into his pocket, removed a small, brown vial. "Give me your hand," he said.

Caraglo reached out with his right hand. Morton removed the cap from the vial, and emptied two tablets into Caraglo's palm.

"Close your hand," he said.

"What's this?" Caraglo asked.

"Please tell the guard I'm leaving now," Dirk answered.

Caraglo pressed the intercom's send button. "Messenger's leaving now," he said.

"Yessir," the guard answered.

At the door of the office, Dirk turned to look at Caraglo. Gabriel "Archangel" Caraglo's head was slumping slowly toward the writing pad on his desk. His eyes on Dirk's face. His lips pursed as he tried to ask: "Why?"

Outside, Morton Dirk looked up at the sky and took four deep breaths...Telamon. Looked for the Hunter's Belt in the Orion constellation. Three stars in a perfectly straight line.... Telamon. The hunter drove home, thinking of the hydrogen furnaces that speckled the sky south of the airport. In the north, the city lights had turned the sky a dark orange.... Telamon. Telamon. Telamon.

Telamon had killed his parents. Why send him to kill Caraglo? Didn't make sense. There was a chance that he would have got the truth from Caraglo. Maybe Telamon believed that Caraglo's death would be swift—coming before Caraglo knew why he was about to die. But there was always the possibility that the target would speak. Telamon did not make mistakes. He knew Morton would discover that Caraglo did not send the men who killed his parents. Why? And if Morton sought revenge by killing the judge, the Organization would finish him. They had known about him long before his parents' deaths. They had killed his parents to get him. They had given him what he had asked for—the death of the man he had held responsible for the two deaths. They now owned him completely—to the point where they could tell him with impunity that they had killed his parents—two imbeciles—unworthy of such a son. In return they had given him power, wealth, and a new parent. And Caraglo, the only other person who could link Telamon to an enterprise, was dead.

Put those thoughts away. Think of the stars and their fire. At the right time—not now—he would kill Telamon. And Hall. And John. And the guards at the mansion. And the Mountries. And the Filipina maid. And the Mexican gardener. And Point—especially Point—who had scarcely deigned to look at him while he ordered his mother and father shot. He would slice the bastard's throat and look into the bastard's eyes until the bastard's eyes dulled. Then he would burn down the mansion. Let the others come after him. He would destroy the entire Organization.

But not yet. Get some sleep. Classes to prepare for: Shakespeare and the John Donne.... Clear the mind. Clear the mind. Wait for the moment. He would confront Telamon face to face. Patience. Patience. Face to face, face to face.

Suddenly he was thinking of Boston and Georgia Enoch. He was actually missing her. He imagined telling her what he had discovered about Caraglo and Telamon and his parents' death; and to ask what he should do. She would probably listen carefully, ask him to let her think about it, and at the first opportunity probably betray him to Telamon. But he still missed her. The only woman who knew who and what he was.

The loneliness came again fast and hard: no friends or family. His only repeated contacts were students and the men at the shelter–and the latter to be kept at a distance. That was easy with the men who walked off the streets lost and angry: they were not interested in making friends either. The jokes and brief conversations were gratuities for the shelter and food. Then their eyes would drift out of focus, faces go blank, and their conversations would be reserved for themselves or for the private voices that came at moments of quiet.

He thought of Millie Vance for a moment: she owed him. For the next thirty minutes he toyed with a scenario of seduction. Until he recalled her tear-streaked face, her skin gray and cold, her hands trembling, blood running down her legs. She would want him to reassure her that she was not being used; that he did not consider her damaged and easy. He forgot about Millie Vance. Tried to imagine the face of Jude Delaware's wife, forcing the image to be beautiful.

All those faces pouring through his mind. He had been generous and good to people who posed no threat to him or to his employers. He was certainly good enough for Jude's wife. Suddenly, he was laughing—incredulous that what he longed for was to take care of somebody. He let the laughter die. His eyes focused on the license plate of the car ahead of him. Indiana. Driver invisible behind the pile of clothes and boxes in the back seat. Another new face in the city. Morton pointed with his right index finger at where the driver's head would be. "Pow," he said. So easy.

He thought again of Augustus Telamon; his lips mouthed words silently: *"For now we see through a glass, darkly; but then face to face."*

7

October, eight years later, and thirty more killings around the country. No connections between the deaths: the police reports said suicide, natural causes, accidents, and three homicides attributed to intruders. Two men were arrested and charged with a couple of the murders. No trace of suspicion hinted at the professor of literature at Charteris University in Atlanta. The Organization operated at its usual level of efficiency.

It had selected an obscure high-school graduate and turned him into one of the most efficient assassins in the United States—perhaps in the world. He sometimes wondered—not very often—whether the Organization was preparing him for something else: Perhaps, as Telamon's successor—when the latter died. One a brilliant judge; his replacement, a brilliant scholar. Pillars of society. Or perhaps he would be discarded when his efficiency diminished. Morton doubted that sentimentality affected the decisions of the Organization; or that it had ever made a misstep.

Or that the Organization had murdered anyone. True, he had been sent to kill several people who had endangered or impeded the Organization's progress. But his actions were different—not the contemptible, meaningless carnage treasured by the local television news editors: Sudden acts of extreme violence by bewildered failures who had surrendered to uncontainable rages at themselves; incapable of understanding their own actions or the consequences: police, arrest, lawyers, courts, sentences, and prisons, executions; shielded from fear by their on opacities. Angry at the world's anger at their anger.

He was not one of those people. He was a scholar: clean, modest, unremarkable but well dressed. He walked without distress in crowed malls, surrounded by people with their own tight secrets. No eyes settled casually on him, then hesitated to wonder whether he could be connected to the murder mentioned on the national news last evening.

The knowing that he was a killer—many times over—free and respected, gave him such an intense sexual arousal that he allowed it only when he was seated or wore a coat long enough to hide his reaction. But not often: he did not want the sharpness of his pleasure dulled by habituation. He was not a murderer.

And eight years after Caraglo's removal, he was preparing to travel to Houston to complete a task for the Organization.

On Sunday night, his telephone rang again at ten o'clock, precisely. Ring, wait, ring, answer. The same old ritual.

"Come see me tomorrow afternoon. At the office, I won't be home until late."

"Yes…Dad."

He parked in the Underground Center parking lot, and walked three blocks to the Supreme Court. Smiled at the policeman standing at the metal detector at the entrance of the hall to the judges offices. "Judge Telamon," he said, "I'm Morton Dirk.

"Yes. Must be his son? He said you'd be coming by this afternoon."

"Yes. Thanks." Put his keys and watch in plastic bowl; retrieved them, and went down the hall. Judge August W. Telamon.

He knocked on the door—three taps, and went in. Judge Telamon rose. Very black and overwhelming: six foot four, a trim two hundred pounds moving like a ballet dancer, graying hair brushed back severely, perfectly round face without a wrinkle, laughing dark-brown eyes. Large mouth smiling...always smiling, even when the light in his eyes died. Gold rimmed glasses on a button of a nose. And two very small round ears. Always in the same colors: tailored pinstripe charcoal-gray suit, black cap-toe oxfords, white shirt, dark tie. Red pocket handkerchief.

"Good afternoon, Dad."

"Hello, Morton. Looking fine as usual. Must be hard on your admirers. Staying fit?"

"I'm well."

"Good. I asked you to come here instead of coming to the house because the information came in this morning and I'm going out of town this evening. And...I suppose it's important to maintain some appearances. You understand...dutiful son visiting father, and so on. Anyway, this job carries a hundred thousand obligation to you."

Judge Telamon looked at Dirk's eyes sweeping the room. "You worry too much. I still have this place checked daily for bugs...then I do it myself again. Anyway, I want you to leave Friday evening, and you should be able to get back here on Sunday. The password is '2-marigold-2.'"

He pushed a twelve-by-six-inch manila envelope across his desk. "It's generous, as usual...ticket, etcetera are inside." Telamon smiled and leaned back in his chair. "You really do take good care of yourself. Very proud of you. Will check with you next Sunday night. Perhaps, later, you can tell me what has been bothering you lately. Perhaps it may be best for us to discuss it."

"I shall speak with you next Sunday," Morton said, and left the room.

On his way out, the guard at the entrance nodded. "Hope you didn't do anything to upset the old man...he'd take it out on us."

Dirk grinned. "You'd better take sick leave then, I just pissed him off royally. Just joking. See you."

"Take care."

He drove to the Farmers' Market east of the city, and bought ten pounds of tuna and grouper steaks, a pound each of shrimp and scallops, and a handful of Scotch bonnet hot peppers. Stopped at the grocery for a new loofa sponge, a package of disposable razors, a package of unscented laundry powder, and a large bar of chocolate with nuts and raisins—his last luxury for the week.

It was five o'clock. Two hours working-out to sweat away the smell of spices in his system; cook something simple; start calming down; forget about Dad; get enough sleep; study the information on the diskette—tomorrow night and every night until he left for Houston.

That evening for dinner he broiled a steak of tuna that he had marinated in a paste of lime juice, black pepper, olive oil, and a quarter of one of the hot chilies. He piled that on the steamed brown rice. Ate a carrot and broccoli salad—just a sprinkling of mixed seasoning; no garlic or onions. Then he showered; scrubbed his body hard, and rubbed on unscented lotion before going to bed at nine. Gave himself time to find something to take his thoughts away from Judge Telamon; hoped the pain from the pepper would sweat away the picture of August Telamon the adopter, the great, the eminent, the generous, the respected, the benevolent, who would have had the governorship of Georgia forced upon him if he were not black.

And August Telamon would have refused; and also would have refused an appointment to the Supreme Court of the United States. If he could have been persuaded to express his most profound regret, it would be that in sixteen years, he had not heard Morton say: "Dad," without hesitation. He truly loved his adopted son.

The information on the computer screen described the most successful real estate developer in Harris county, Texas. And Mallon Stanza's acquisitiveness had made him an impediment to the Organization's plans in Houston.

Target: Six foot, six inches tall; three hundred pounds. Ferocious temper; resemblance to late actor Errol Flynn.

Beretta in rear holster, smaller pistol in right ankle holster. Knife in left ankle sheath.

Ex-marine; kick-boxing afficionado and expert.

Mistress in a luxury home owned by Stanza in northwest Houston. Letitia Tsai, Chinese Portugese from Macao, China; strikingly beautiful, used to be married to former employee of Mallon Stanza. Husband paid half a million dollars to divorce her—amicably.

Stanza and Tsai have dinner in a private room at Tuna's, a bay side restaurant in Clear Lake City every third Saturday night. Stanza spends entire night with Tsai, goes home in late afternoon in time for Sunday dinner. This is his only ritual.

Wife resigned to situation; prenuptial agreement ensures her loyalty.

The diskette continued with details of Stanza's temperament, speech, automobile; details of his mistress's house; directions to the house; escape routes; and the telephone number of the Organization's contact in Houston—in the unlikely event that something went wrong.

The last lines of instructions read:

"Safe parking at Karlsson's Restaurant at 354 Fiera Road, one mile south of house.

Area heavily treed with live oaks.

Access only through back yard.

Security light disabled by cleaning service.

Code for the security system at house is '13329.'

Occupants should arrive between 21:30 and 22:00 hours."

Morton looked at the photos of his targets. A remarkably handsome couple. Even the digital photograph could not diminish the beauty of the woman. He could understand how a man could leave his wife for such a face; or write poetry to it; or fall in love with it more deeply every day. After he killed her, he would spend a few minutes enjoying the beauty of Letitia Tsai.

The envelope that had held the diskette also contained one thousand dollars in cash, an airline ticket to Hobby Airport, a credit card, a driver's licence with a photograph of a man who looked vaguely like him, an insurance certificate, and two house keys.

He called a car-rental agency to reserve a car in Houston.

Friday evening at Hobby Airport. October still warm and humid. Morton wore khaki slacks, a white knit shirt, and a tan linen sports jacket. He carried an overnight bag containing a black jogging suit made of thin black cotton, a toiletry kit, black running shoes, a change of underwear, black latex gloves, a two-inch long flashlight with a ring for a key chain, and a thick file of students' papers.

He went to the rental car counter. "Car for Christopher?" He presented a driver's licence, insurance card, and a credit card with the name: Charles P. Christopher.

The auburn-haired woman behind the counter tapped his name into her computer.

"For two days, Mr. Christopher? Economy, medium or large car, sir?" she asked.

"Economy, please. How far to Galveston?"

"Oh…thirty miles…forty minutes, sir. South on I-45."

"Not bad," he said.

"Visiting? Business?" the woman asked. Obligatory pleasantries.

"Visiting. Friend in hospital there," Morton said.

"Sorry to hear that. Hope your friend gets better soon."

"Thanks," said the man with the unremarkable face.

Fifteen minutes later, he drove out of the car-rental parking lot and turned north on the access road to Highway 45, North. A mile further on, he pulled into a shopping mall and stopped near a department store. Looked at the store directory near the escalator and went up to the third floor—kitchenware. He picked up a filleting knife.

"Going hunting?" the clerk at the cash register asked.

"Nope. Fishing in Galveston Bay," Morton answered.

"Gee, can I come along?"

"Sure," Morton said. He paid and took the boxed knife. "Thanks."

"Enjoy," the man said.

Morton looked around for a bookstore. None. He found a pharmacy. Picked up a map of Houston and its suburbs.

In the car, he turned on the reading lamp and located Fiera Road. It was seven thirty-six. Already dark. Still early. He stopped at a motel near the junction of I-45 and the 610 Loop. He showered, using his own soap, and changed into the black tracksuit. Next, he pulled the khaki slacks and jacket over the tracksuit. He returned to the car with the briefcase. He slid the knife into the space between he cushion and back rest of his seat. Should take him forty-five minutes to get to Karlsson's.

Ten minutes past nine. He turned west on the 610 South Loop Freeway. Went through the list on the diskette, visualized the house, his movements, heard the sounds of the targets, even his own breathing...then every move until his exit from the house. Looked at possible unexpected events. And countermeasures for the certainty that something that would go wrong. Anticipate every possible eventuality. Anticipate, anticipate. Then do it all over.

He was focused on his entry into the victims' bedroom, when the blue lights of a police cruiser flickered in his rear-view mirror. Couldn't be...he was driving at the speed limit. The speedometer needle indicated 45. He pulled over. Waited.

"Evening, sir. Having a bit of a problem? Your speed's been going from forty to sixty. Can I see your licence and proof of insurance, please?" The policeman looked like a six-foot eight-inch tall barrel, and as hard. Sunburned. Face as round, mottled, and red as a pizza. No expression.

Morton handed over the cards. "I'm sorry. Trying to get my bearings."

"Where're you headed to, sir?"

"Galveston."

"Galveston? That's in the other direction...south. You're going north." He shone his flashlight into the back seat. "What do you have there, sir. Can I have a look? Please step out of the car, sir. And place your hands on the roof. Thank you." The policeman opened the back door and took out the small black suitcase. He opened it. "What are these papers, sir?"

"Student reports," Morton said.

"You're some sort of college professor in...?" He looked at the licence, "Atlanta, Georgia?"

"Yes, sir."

"What the hell you doing, lost in Houston?"

"Thought I'd take a short holiday in Galveston. Thought it'd be nice to get away from the class for a couple, three days," Morton said.

"And you took papers to correct? Hotdamn'. Man, you're dedicated. They don't pay teachers half enough for the work they do." The policeman was grinning.

"I hear it's the same for the police," Morton said.

"Damn' right, it is. If you love your job, that's what they going to pay you with...love. Look, you drive on a couple miles more and turn around at the Northwest Parkway. Take the I-45 going south to Galveston. Enjoy your holiday." He handed Morton's licence and insurance cards back. "Son-of-a-gun," he said, "I sure wouldn't take my work on holiday." He returned to his car. "Watch your speed, now, Professor."

Morton exited at the Northwest Freeway and drove west along the freeway for five miles. Turned right at Fiera Road. Pulled into Karlsson's, drove into the back, and parked between a car and a van. Waited for ten minutes. No police car. No one else came into the back parking lot. He waited for his breathing and heart to slow. First time he had made a mistake...and the last time. A few more seconds—and the episode with the policeman was forgotten. He slipped off the jacket and slacks. Put the knife into a pouch strapped to the inside of his arm. He tied the keys to Tsai's house and the flashlight to a string and looped that around his neck. Pulled on a pair of black latex gloves.

The shadow set off for Tsai's home. Keeping to the edge of the sidewalk away from the road. Alert for car lights. Ready to jump between the oak trees. No cars, no dogs barking. Just crickets complaining about the cold. He found the house, ran past, dodged into the woods nearby, and doubled back toward the rear of the house. Walked in a straight line to the back door. The house remained dark. He unlocked the door and entered the kitchen. Turned on the small flashlight. The alarm began beeping urgently. Morton went to the red light flashing from a box near the door leading to the garage. He entered the code and the alarm went silent. He sniffed the air. Letitia Tsai did not cook very often; and no smell of pets; just the scent of one perfume. Joy. Very expensive. He shone his pencil light around the room. Four jade vases on pedestals, one at each corner of the living room. Six large oil paintings on the walls; pieces he would have been delighted to own. Wondered whose tastes they reflected. Probably hers. Classy lady. He went quickly up the stairs and found the bedrooms. The guest room was across the hall from the main bedroom. Its door was left open about four inches. Few smells in the guest room—not used for a long time. He examined both rooms and their locks carefully, then went back downstairs to reset the alarm. He went back into the guest room and left the door open exactly as he had found it. Ten seconds.

He was sitting on the floor of the walk-in cupboard when the chirps of the alarm rearming itself stopped. The red figures on clock radio on the dresser near the bed had said 10:30. Morton drew his legs up, put his arms around them and rested his head on his knees. He closed his eyes, and his breathing slowed to his sleep rate. His limbs grew cold. He waited.

He did not move until the alarm beeped again, and stopped. He heard voices and footsteps. Closer. Stopped Outside the guest room. "Should I make some coffee?" the woman asked.

"Nah. Just want some water. I'll get it in the bathroom," the man said. He heard the sounds of the alarm as it was rearmed.

The door of the bedroom opposite opened, and must have remained ajar: he could still hear them. A faint thump, and the woman giggled. "That hurts," she said.

"But feels good."

"For you," Letitia Tsai said.

"This is nice...do it again," Stanza said.

One of them turned the radio on. Jazz music.

"What is Mrs. Mallon Stanza preparing for dinner tomorrow, darling?" Letitia asked.

"No idea, but it will be good," Stanza said.

"You had to get that in, didn't you?"

"You started it, honey-chile."

"Prick," Letitia said.

Silence for a few minutes then a giggle. Bathroom sounds. The bed creaked twice. The music on the radio stopped and started; changed to soft night music. The bead creaked again.

Across the hall, Morton Dirk's heart rate increased from sixty to one eighty beats per minute, and his breathing grew deeper. His circulatory system shunted more blood to his extremities until his hands and feet would have felt feverishly hot to the touch. At that point, he could move with blinding speed— faster than an Olympic sprinter, but for only a few minutes. He must kill quickly.

He rose slowly, until he was standing rigidly upright. He stretched his arms forward and stood on his toes; bent his head from side to side; relaxed, and repeated the movements. Finally, a deep breath. He was ready.

Rhythmic creaking of the bed for ten minutes. Heavy grunting from Mallon Stanza; moans from Letitia Tsai. A deep howl and a thin scream intermingled; then a long sigh. Morton waited for fifteen minutes more then left his hiding place and went out into the hallway, stopped outside the other bedroom and listened. He could hear Mallon's breathing— long and slow; already into deep sleep.

He pushed their door open, a millimeter at a time, until he could see the two bodies intertwined under a thin blanket. Tsai's body was cupped by the enormous curve of her lover. Their faces were turned away from him. He pushed the door open, just wide enough for him to slip into the room. He walked over to the bedside. Mallon Stanza's clothes were hung on the back of a chair. His gun and a small sheathed knife were on the bedside dresser near the clock radio. Dirk walked around to Mallon's side of the bed, the knife already sliding out of his left sleeve.

Stanza's hand shifted slightly under the pillow, and he moved his head as if to adjust to the changed shape of the pillow. Then his hand shot out toward Dirk and there were two bright flashes of orange toward the space where Dirk's chest had been a fraction of a second before. The two-shot Derringer was empty. Just as quickly, the large man was out of bed and lunging for the gun on the bedside table.

Morton's right heel caught Stanza under his jaw, and almost lifted him off the bed. The blow threw him on his back, over the body of Letitia Tsai, who was screaming into a pillow she clutched to her chest. Stanza propelled himself forward, diving for Morton's legs. Again, he missed. Fell on his face. Before Dirk could reach him, Stanza had rolled away. Caught Dirk's left ankle and jerked him off balance. Stanza was on his feet again; lips drawn back, teeth bared for Dirk's neck. He launched himself at Dirk who was still rising from his fall. Dirk bent to the right and his left leg flicked toward Stanza and returned, like the lunge of a praying mantis. The feint caused Stanza to hesitate—time for Dirk's spinning body to send his right heel into Stanza's face. The other man recovered quickly, ducked, and the kick caught him on the shoulder. They circled each other: Morton tiring, Stanza regaining his confidence, edging closer to his gun on the night stand. Letitia sensed his intent, and looked at the gun. Dirk caught her glance. Time to end it. His body sagged, as if in defeat. Stanza saw the hint of surrender. He spun around and his body coiled to spring for the gun. Dirk's foot caught his ankle, throwing the larger man off balance. Stanza tried to crawl to the automatic. Letitia Tsai threw herself toward the night stand.

"No!" the voice stopped her cold, caused her lover to hesitate for a split second—time enough for Dirk to launch himself, feet first into Stanza's side. Stanza rolled to the right, gasping, rose on all fours, and was looking around for the intruder when the knife flashed beneath his throat. He managed to stand, even with his head almost severed. Turned toward his lover, his hands reaching for her help. A second more. And his body folded to the floor.

Letitia Tsai was lying curled up on her side, still clutching the pillow. She tried to scream again, but no sound came. Morton walked over to her side of the bed. He was breathing hard; more from surprise than exhaustion. If Stanza had been more prepared, it would have been a closer fight. He had never seen anyone, not even Point, react so quickly to a sudden unexpected threat. And he was astonished that Mallon Stanza had survived blows that should have killed a normal, healthy man.

The woman put the pillow aside...slowly, and turned to lie on her back. She was now fully exposed. "Please...I will give you anything you want. Please, don't kill me. I'll give you anything. Please...please. I beg you...please."

Morton walked to the bedside table, and turned on the light. For almost a minute he stared at the face and body of Letitia Tsai. Every part of her. Studying her slowly as if he stood alone at a private showing of a great work of art. She was even more beautiful than he had anticipated.

Her breathing became less agitated. She forced herself to become calmer. Perhaps if she let him rape her, he would let her live. She opened her legs. "Please?"

Morton Dirk shook his head. He should kill her quickly and leave...before she saw his arousal. Morton could feel his chest tightening and his legs tingling. He steadied his breathing. "Ms. Tsai, I am grateful for having lived to see a woman as beautiful as you...because I do not think that there is another. For the rest of my life, I shall regret this, but I cannot let you live...not after what you have seen. I am really very, very sorry."

He walked to her side, and brushed her hair away from her face. Pulled her head back to bare her neck. She did not resist; and her eyes had already lost their focus when the blade flashed under her chin.

He went around the bed to Stanza'a body and rolled it on its back with his foot. Bent over, and with the tip of the knife, cut the word "PUERCO," in block capitals on the chest and down the abdomen. Went back to Tsai's corpse and in similar letters starting below her breasts and down to her navel, carved "PUTA." He studied the letters to see whether they carried any of his writing peculiarities. Nothing. Mostly straight short lines.

Before he left the room, he stood at the foot of the bed looking at the exquisite body of Letitia Tsai and the scarlet halo spreading around her head. He wished he were capable of crying for her. Tomorrow, he would tell Augustus Telamon that he would never again kill a woman. Not even in self defense. Nor would he desecrate a corpse again. Never.

He went into the bathroom, rinsed the blood off the knife, and returned it into its sheath.

He went into the guest room and turned on the light. He pulled the blanket and top sheet off one side of the bed. Stood on the bed and walked the length of the mattress; pressed down on the pillow with his gloved fists; then smoothed the individual impressions of his shoes. He went into the bathroom and turned on the faucets in the shower and wash basin. Washed his gloved hands and wiped his hands with the bath and hand towels. Left the bath towel lying in the tub. Pulled the hand towel to the side of its rack, so that it hung askew. He looked around carefully for strands of his hair in the bathroom; made small dishevelments a guest would make; went back to look at the bed; pulled the bottom sheet out an inch at the side and top; turned the light off, and left the room.

He crossed the hallway, and gazed again at the face of Letitia Tsai. Turned the light off and looked around—carefully. Nothing left behind. Looked at the body again, went to it, and touched the hand gently.

At the top of the stairs, he stopped suddenly with his foot inches above the first step. He pulled back slowly. The alarm. He went back into the room and found the remote control near Stanza's gun. He turned the alarm off, and took the control downstairs into the kitchen. Reset it before he left.

He set off jogging toward Karlsson's. Two blocks before the restaurant, he met a couple walking a golden retriever. The dog strained at him. He smiled at the couple. "Nice night," he said.

"Hi," the woman replied. The man nodded.

Morton sensed them looking back at him. He shrugged. They would remember only a black face. And not well enough to pick him out in a line-up one hour from then.

Sixteen hours later, he was driving home from Hartsfield Airport in Atlanta. He was thinking that one could make a reasonable argument that hurricanes were living entities: They grew in size; respired by sucking warm air from the ocean surface; responded to air currents around them; moved across oceans; fed on water vapor; excreted rain; and reproduced–spinning off tornadoes and storms as they died over land masses. He amused himself imagining the thoughts of a hurricane as it considered ways of confounding the humans who tried to predict its behavior. Someday, humans would discover a way of stopping a hurricane–then regret it when the incalculable energy of the storm exploded in another form. That would be an interesting dilemma to pose to a class. Perhaps he could work it into *Oedipus*. Something along the line of a man challenging the fates.

He turned east on I-20. Tomorrow, to Perimeter Mall: Call his bank to hear the singing voice tell him he was one hundred thousand dollars richer. Acknowledge Telamon's compliments...and insist that he would not kill another woman. Visit the men's shelter. Time to talk to Jude's wife. Take her his friend's ashes.

Twenty four hours after Morton Dirk left Houston, Mallon Stanza's wife called the police. She had spent the entire day calling her husband's telephone numbers in his office and car; and his pager. She called his secretary and all his staff members and friends whose numbers she could find. The secretary called every number on her Rolodex file. No, no one had seen, or heard from the boss since Saturday. Candace Mallon gave Letitia Tsai's address to the police.

A policewoman arrived at her home forty seven minutes later to tell her they had found the body of her husband…with the body of Letitia Tsai. They had both been murdered.

Five hours later, the media got the story. A couple who lived half a mile from Letitia Tsai's house, telephoned the police to say they had seen a black man jogging in the area. They had not seen his face clearly, but were surprised to see a black person jogging in that neighborhood at one o'clock in the morning. The papers also reported that the bodies had been mutilated with the words "pig" and "prostitute" carved in Spanish on their abdomens.

When Officer Coty Amsterdam saw the report he remembered the black man he had stopped near the Northwest Parkway exit. The teacher going the wrong way to Galveston. But the man had been wearing a tan jacket and khaki slacks, not a black jogging suit. And the report said that there had not been any sign of a forced entry. The alarm had not gone off. The guest bed had been slept in. Stanza and his mistress must have been killed by someone they had invited into the house. And their guest was certainly not a black male teacher going the wrong way to Galveston with a briefcase full of students' papers to correct. Amsterdam tried to recall the teacher's face. Nothing. He remembered the name: Christopher. Not Hispanic. Killer? Nope. No way. No how.

The police sent two detectives to interview the Costa Rican husband of Letitia Tsai in San José, Costa Rica. They wanted to talk with any Chinese or Hispanic businessman or businesswoman who had some reason to hate Mallon Stanza. In four days, they compiled a list of one hundred and seventy nine names.

8

In Atlanta, Judge Telamon telephoned Morton at ten, exactly. "Excellent," he said. "My information tells me the police are interviewing several of the couple's friends and associates. I shall obtain a copy of the Houston Chronicle. When shall we see you again? I have not heard one of your class lectures for a long time. What are your students tackling now?"

"They've discovered that poetry can be sexy," Morton replied.

"Romantic stuff?" Telamon asked

"No. Salacious," Morton said.

There was a long silence before the judge spoke again. "Come have dinner soon. I'll make sure there's bread pudding."

Morton did not sleep well that night. He awoke at one o'clock shivering from a nightmare in which he had been chasing the headless body of Letitia Tsai through the streets of Atlanta, trying to replace her laughing head. Her blood ran unceasingly down his arms to his elbows, and splashed against his thighs and legs. He tried to hide his face by keeping his head bowed, but the crowds at the side of the road recognized him, shouting: "Morton Dirk…Morton Dirk…murderer…poet." In the dream, he tried pleading with the fleeing corpse to stop. But the head laughed at him. Laughed until tears flowed from its eyes.

For several minutes he sat up in bed breathing hard. Perhaps he needed a vacation. Perhaps he should take a year off working for Telamon. The thought lasted only a few seconds—he would be fine as soon as the sun rose. But he was unable to fall asleep again.

In the afternoon, he was too tired to call the offshore bank to ask about the latest deposit to his account. Too tired for anything. Too tired for sex at a motel rendezvous. Too tired to talk to the superintendent at the shelter about Jude's wife. Tomorrow.

On Tuesday afternoon, he felt better. Still not enough sleep, but more than the night before. He was in his office, and was dialing the number for the shelter when someone knocked softly on his door. "Come in," he said.

"Hello, Prof," Gaynor Franklyn said.

"Hello, Gaynor. Come, sit down. Anything wrong?"

"Not with me, but you didn't look too good in class today. You're okay?"

"Yes, yes, fine. Had a nightmare last night. Couldn't sleep."

"You always seem to have these bad nights on Sundays. I suspect you must be doing something really interesting on the weekends."

"Cleaning? Laundry? Groceries? Yes...really interesting," he replied.

"Want to see me again? You don't have to give me anything. I'm just a little...frisky," Gaynor said.

"You're such a blessing," Morton said. You always seem to know when I want...I don't know...relief?"

"Why don't you have a regular girlfriend, Prof?" she asked.

"How do you know that I don't?"

"I can tell."

"How?"

"You put too much into it. If you were getting it regularly, you wouldn't be able to go three times...each time," Gaynor Franklyn replied.

"You're too smart for my tired mind this afternoon."

"So, when do you want to see me again? Those last lectures of yours have been driving me crazy. After the first one, the one with the poem by Elmira Agustini? The whole class went to the bathroom. And some of us were in there for longer that it took to pee. During the class, I wanted to put my hand between my legs so bad."

"For heaven's sake, Gaynor," he said.

"No, really, Prof. If you wanted it now, I'd give it to you on the desk. Right now…if you asked for it. It's that voice of yours…and the way you took care of Millie."

"She told you?"

"Can't keep a thing like that to yourself, you know."

"Apparently," Morton said.

"Did she give you anything in return?"

"No, she did not. That's not why I helped."

"I know…just jealous. I want you so bad, Morton. Want to do it?"

"Here? Are you crazy?"

"I don't care," Gaynor said.

"What I need now, is a tray of ice cubes. But I have so much to do. I may be away this weekend…friend's funeral in Denver. But afterwards? Soon as I get back?"

"I'll be ready," Gaynor Franklyn said.

"Need anything?" Morton asked.

"Yeah, but it looks like I'll have to wait for it," she said, and went to the door. She stopped, remembering something she had hesitated to ask: "One morning, you made us read famous first lines, and I went on and on…something strange happened to me that morning: I could hear the words before I spoke them. And, you won't believe this, but I had and orgasm. It was short, but it was a real orgasm. I was soaked. Know something, I'm sure you did it. Don't know how, but you did it, Morton Dirk. And I wish I knew how, so I could do it again…all day long. Tell me, did you do that?"

"I remember wishing I could be making love while you read to me, but that's all. I don't do ESP," Morton answered.

"You're a weird guy, Professor Dirk, and I suspect I should be scared to hell of you. But I can't let go." She walked back to the door, looked back. "If you asked me, I'd tell you that I love you, Morton…even if I had to share with somebody else."

Gaynor closed the door slowly behind her, as if to give him time to call her back. The door clicked shut.

Morton was grateful for the distraction. For several minutes, he gazed at the door, trying to maintain her image: Five feet, eight inches of brown. Skin brown and smooth as chocolate with a touch of cream, brown hair streaked with gold, dark-brown eyes, a nose that crinkled when she laughed, small hips and breasts, and lips in full pout. Usually, black slacks and silk sweaters. Elegant as a cheetah. He would miss her when she left at the end of the spring semester. But there would be another. Probably by the third class.

At that moment, he had to deal with Jude's remains and his wife. He called the men's shelter. The superintendent answered.

"Hey, Dr. Dirk, good to hear from you again. Yes, I got in touch with Jude's wife…after about four days. So, I had gone ahead and asked the funeral home to cremate the body."

"How did she take it. His death and the cremation?"

"She didn't sound too surprised; but I could tell it hurt her. She was surprised he was in Atlanta. Thought he had gone to Miami. He used to talk about wanting to live somewhere hot…near the ocean."

"And the cremation?" Morton asked.

"She said she understood. She was going to fly down to collect the remains, but I told her to wait until I spoke with you. Told her you were Jude's best friend. She couldn't understand when I told her you were a college professor. Asked me if you were for real. She didn't say it, but I could tell she wanted to know if you were…you know," the superintendent said.

"I guess I'd feel the same way," Morton replied.

"Yep. Can't even do a person a favor, these days. Nothing for nothing."

"Yes," Morton said. "May I have her telephone number, please? I'll call her tonight."

"Here you are...."

Morton called at eleven. Nine o'clock in Denver. "Mrs. Delaware?"

"Yes?"

"My name is Dr. Morton Dirk, I am calling a...."

"The professor of literature," Colette Delaware said. "I was waiting for your call."

"Thank you, Mrs. Delaware...or is it Dr. Delaware? Jude said you were a science professor."

"Mrs." she said, "I have a Master's in biology. I teach Grade Twelve science...Everton High School."

"I see. Mrs. Delaware, I would like to bring Jude's remains to Denver. I think it would be too much for you to travel here and back for that purpose. It would not be pleasant trip. And I had promised Jude."

"Dr. Dirk...I need to ask you this: Why? Jude was...a...a homeless alcoholic. What did you two have in common? I'm sorry to sound ungrateful, but this is very..."

"Strange?" Morton asked.

"Yes."

"One afternoon, Jude walked into my class, unannounced, said that he had heard about my fame, and wanted help writing a book on his experiences. Security took him out very quickly, before I could answer. Anyway, I did ask him where I could find him. On impulse. Probably because I didn't know what to do. So, I did meet him in a park. I actually thought it would be a worthwhile project, working with him on his life. But he had lost interest by then. Said there were too many bums around. Who wanted to read about them after seeing them all day? So, I used to drop in now and then to see him at the men's shelter. Jude's philosophy about everything was...I'm sorry...but it was hilarious. Then, I started volunteering at the shelter, collecting bits of unusual humor and opinions from the men who came there. I do not yet have a family, and that may part of the reason for going there. That's all. I'm a very conventional person."

"The man who called me from the shelter said about the same thing," Colette said, "but, you know, it was unusual."

"Yes, Ma'am, I understand. I would like to know, though, whether you would permit me to bring his ashes to Denver."

"Mr.—Dr. Dirk, I cannot impose that on you, I...."

"Please? It would be my last favor to Jude. He wanted me to say something nice about him to you. Some 'good shit,' was the way he put it."

Morton heard her laugh slightly, and heard the sniffle too.

"How long will you be staying? Do you want me to book a hotel room for you?"

"Yes, please. I'll call you tomorrow with the flight information. Will probably be Friday evening."

"I'll pick you up from the airport, if you like," Colette Delaware said.

"Yes please, that would be very good. Goodbye, Mrs. Delaware."

"Goodbye, and thanks, Dr. Dirk."

He called back on Thursday evening to tell Colette Delaware that he would be arriving on United Airlines, at six in the evening. She gave him the name of the hotel where she had made a reservation for him; and read him the reservation number. He caught the trace of excitement in her voice. Or curiosity.

"I'll meet you in the baggage claim. I'll be standing under the winged gargoyle near Exit five-oh-six."

"Are you sure that's not too much trouble? I could take a shuttle or taxi to the hotel," he said.

"No, Dr. Dirk, after all that you did for Jude, this is hardly sufficient thanks."

"I shall see you tomorrow, then, Mrs. Delaware. Goodbye."

Twenty two and a half hours later, he rode the escalator down to the baggage claim. Saw the gargoyle directly ahead, and the woman dressed almost formally in a black wool coat, opened to show a long skirt split to the knee, and a white turtle neck sweater. She had dressed to intimidate and impress him. As different from Jude as she could make herself. Her hair was pulled back and tied in a bun. And she was prettier than he had hoped for. A serene oval face with eyes slanted downwards, and a very round mouth. There was a mole midway between the right corner of her mouth and her chin; and a chain of freckles that arced under her right eye and stretched to the bridge of her nose. She was the same mid-brown complexion as Jude.

Her eyes caught Morton's and moved on, still searching, probably looking for something more exciting. She stood very still; her hands clasped at the front; only her eyes moving. He walked slowly toward her, and only when he was ten feet away did her eyes stop at his face. Went over his clothes: conservative and obviously expensive. A tiny frown. "Dr. Dirk?"

He nodded, extended his hand. "Very pleased to meet you, Mrs. Delaware. And thanks for meeting me."

"Pleased to meet you, Dr. Dirk. I'm very grateful for…all your trouble. Did you have a good flight?"

"Yes, very. Touched down on the minute."

"Good." She looked at his garment bag and carry-on case. "Any other luggage to collect?"

"That's it," he said. He nodded at the carry-on. She understood.

"Okay then, my car's a ten-minute walk away. Can I help you with anything."

"No, no," he said. And he could tell that she was relieved.

In the car, she said: "Should I stop at my home to leave the remains before I took you to your hotel? I think you've spent enough time with my husband." She pursed her lips to hide the smile.

"Is it going to make you uncomfortable?" he asked.

"Not anymore, I've had a couple days to prepare for it. I'll be fine. And it would be too much to ask you to keep it in your room. Is it in an urn?"

"Yes," Morton answered.

"You mind coming with me to the funeral home tomorrow? I've already made the arrangements. A couple of his relatives will be there," Called said.

"The least I could do," Morton said.

"Thanks again," she said.

The house looked like an Alpine cottage, made of brown and red sandstone, with white trim. A small flower bed on each side of the front steps. Everything neat and symmetrical. He suspected that the fall leaves hesitated to sully her lawn. He followed her into the kitchen from the garage. Smells of cinnamon and citrus and vanilla.

"You bake a lot?" Morton asked.

"Yes, I like making pastries. Mostly for friends. I prefer eating other people's baking. But I like the smells and the effort; and looking at the results. Do you cook, Dr. Dirk?"

"Please call me Morton. The Doctor thing is embarrassing."

"And I'm Colette," she said.

"Good. Yes, I like cooking. But not sweets. Basic stuff like meats and fish. I make a recognizable coq-au-vin."

"That's one of the dishes I know only by mention. Never had it."

"Oh, and I make an exceptional bread pudding…with a bourbon sauce. The only sweet I do make. And I promise you with all modesty, it's really good. Got the recipe from my adoptive father's cook."

"You're adopted? What…?"

"My parents died in a car accident, when I was quite young. Don't remember them. I was adopted by a close friend of my parents. A judge who had lost his wife. Didn't have children. Sent me to Harvard. He's comfortable."

"You were fortunate," Colette said.

"Yes, indeed," Morton said.

He opened the black case and removed a twelve inch high cedar box. "The urn's in here. Where shall I put it?" he asked. "I don't know…the mantel piece, I suppose. That's where I think it's kept." She did not seem anxious to take the box from him.

Morton placed the box near the fireplace. He noticed the art covering the walls; and the wood, bronze, and stone sculptures on every table, and on small pedestals. Later, he would ask her about it.

"Do you want to freshen up, or anything, Morton?" she asked.

"May I use the bathroom, please?"

She led him out of the living room.

When he returned, she was holding her car keys. "Ready?" she asked.

She did not say much on the way to the hotel. Morton supposed she was hesitant to return and share the house with her husband's ashes. He had thought of asking her whether he could stay. Sleep on the couch in the living room. Too early. She still did not know what to make of him. He had seen her look curiously at him in the living room as if she could not retain the image of his face in her memory.

At the hotel, he asked whether she would stop in for coffee. She seem relieved. "It's too late for coffee, for me. But I'd like a soda and a snack. Didn't have time to eat. I'm sorry, I completely forgot to ask if you were hungry. Are you?"

"Not yet, but will be in a couple hours. Why don't we have dinner here?"

"If you let me treat you," Colette said.

"On a teacher's salary?" he asked.

"You can have a packet of crackers," she said. This time she allowed the smile.

Morton looked at her transformed face and cursed Jude Delaware for an idiot. He congratulated himself for asking her to stay.

They both had small salads, and salmon chowder with toast. Morton asked for hot chocolate, and she did the same when she caught the scent of chocolate and nutmeg. "Always reminds me of Christmas," she said.

When the table was cleared, Morton said, "Colette, Jude wanted me to say something nice about himself when I did see you. He did not tell me what to say, and I know little about his life. What I do remember, is that he admired you enormously, and....I suspect that he felt intimidated by you. But he never said a bad thing about you."

Colette Delaware looked directly into his eyes as if reading the words as he spoke. Took a deep breath. "Jude was an alcoholic when I met him. But he has such a joy for beautiful things. His first words to me...the first time I met him, crossing a field on campus, was that he would be satisfied to spend the rest of the day sitting on the hill looking at me. Corny, but the way he said it...made my legs weak. I wanted to take his hand and drag him to my apartment. And that's how it was, for the year we went out together, before we got married. The man made me feel I could walk on water. I spent a lot of money on clothes so I would always look good for him. And, without boasting, we really were a good looking couple. In return, he tried to remain sober. But I could see his hands tremble...and his face sweat, when we were out together and he couldn't have a drink. I was still convinced I could change him.

"After we got married, he tried, but couldn't manage. And it affected other things. Our sex lives were...well, let's say there was little intimacy because his drinking affected him that way. I didn't reproach him at first, but I guess the failure humiliated him...especially as I was not...sexually repressed. After two years, I began pressuring him to get treatment. He tried and failed, tried and failed. Then he became resentful. Said some really dumb things to me. One night I told him there was more to life than breathing stinking fumes of alcohol in bed every night. He went to sleep in the living room. When I got home that afternoon, he was gone. Not a word for five years, until I got the call from Atlanta. Of course his relatives blamed me for his drinking. Said...the usual."

"What did Jude do?" Morton asked.

"He was a commercial artist. Did the most popular billboards in Denver...when he was sober. His firm kept him only because of his skill. I have photographs of his works. I'd like to show them to you if you have time," Colette said.

"He never mentioned that to anyone at the shelter."

"Was probably afraid that someone would ask him to paint and then see that his hands shook too much. Poor Jude."

A few minutes later she began making preparations to leave. "When are you returning to Atlanta?" she asked.

"Tomorrow morning," he said.

"Couldn't you change to a later flight? I'd like to show you a bit of Denver before you left. It wouldn't be fair to have come all this way, and not have done something relaxing. It's up to you."

Morton grinned. "I was hoping for a chance to suggest that. I can call the airline when I get to my room. If you don't mind, I'd like to stay until Sunday afternoon. Would you have time, though?"

"Of course," she said. "I'll see you tomorrow. The service for Jude is at eight. I hesitate now to ask you to attend…because I will have to explain you to his relatives. So, call me when you're ready. I should be home by ten. She took a card out of her handbag. Wrote her home telephone number on the back. "I'm up early, anyway," she said.

Morton walked her to her car. She was different from the solemn lady he had met at the airport. Almost danced to the car. Morton guessed that it was a long time since she had gone out with another man…and had been able to relax. He was happy that she had yielded so easily. He knew that if he had asked to sleep with her, she would gladly have taken him home with her, thinking she had done it on her own volition.

Later, in bed, he wondered whether he should enjoy her before he went back. The usual three times. Not yet. After all these years with Jude, and with his memory, she deserved a holiday. That was it: he would give her the best holiday of her life. Make her forget Jude. Bring her to Atlanta. Then the Caribbean, Hawaii, Europe. His first romantic date. It would be fascinating playing at being in love. And when Gaynor Franklyn graduated, there would be no urgency for a replacement. Life was good.

He pictured Augustus Telamon's face when the bastard found out. Morton would take her to Sunday dinner at the judge's.

Telamon.... There was no place in the Organization for distractions like romance or attachments or obligations or sentiment. Kiss my butt, Telamon.

She picked him up from the hotel at noon.

"How was it?" Morton asked.

"A good service. I think everyone parted on cordial terms."

"Good," I was worried all morning.

"Thanks, Morton. Morton?"

He turned toward her.

"Are you really that sweet a person...or are you feeling sorry for me...because of Jude?"

"What an embarrassment," Morton said. "I'm only reciprocating your kindness, Colette."

"Please, don't be so formal with me. But you really are a sweet guy. I can understand why Jude liked you. He wouldn't have met many people like you, I'm sure." After a pause, she asked suddenly: "Are you married, Morton?"

"No, not yet. Last girlfriend found someone more exciting," Morton said.

"Silly girl. Anyway, I'm glad. Now, I can flirt with you for a day...without getting into trouble," Colette Delaware said.

"You learned well from Jude—all that smart talk," Morton said. "Now, I want to walk on water for you, climb tall mountains, buy you Tiffany's. Any prize you want me to get you?"

"Not right now, the company's good enough. Now, here's a tourist brochure I picked up in the hotel lobby. Let's see what you'd like to visit."

"May I?" Morton scanned the brochures. "Old West, cowboys, railroads, buffalo hunts, railroads.... Here's something interesting. Didn't know a third of cowboys were black."

"That always catches the eye," Colette said. "It's the Black American West Museum. Want to go?"

"Sure. And this looks good too: Museo de las Americas," Morton said.

"Haven't been there. Do you speak Spanish, Morton?" she asked.

"I don't suppose that will be a requirement for entry. Just joking, just joking. But yes, I know enough to obtain board and lodging in a Spanish-speaking city."

"Show off," Colette said.

Visits to two museums and an art gallery took up the rest of the day. It was already dark when Morton suggested a restaurant.

"No, let me cook you dinner," Colette said.

"Got a better idea, let's both cook dinner. I'll do the meat, you can do the vegetables and a dessert."

"What are you going to do?"

"Coq-au-vin, naturally. Why do you think I mentioned it before?" Morton said.

"Professor Dirk, let me ask you something: Do you read people's minds; or do you make people do what you want? There's something very persuasive about you. And I think it's your voice."

"I am a teacher, remember? And you probably do the same thing," Morton said.

"Not as well as you, though. Yes, I think it's your voice. Makes me so comfortable. Morton?"

"Yes, Colette"

"You wouldn't be trying to seduce me, would you? Because it's been a very long time for me, and I wouldn't put up much of a struggle; but I don't want to be used. You understand?"

"I don't work that way, Colette. I came here because of a promise to a friend. I had no idea what you were like, and so did not come prepared for anything, good or bad. If it would make you more comfortable, I'll leave on the next plane…with good thoughts of you."

"What do you think of me, Morton?"

"A gem. A very precious gem. A woman like you needs to be treasured. I think that's what Jude meant when he said he could spend all day looking at you."

"That's exactly what I meant about you. Now, I'm all weak-kneed and absolutely vulnerable. I...I wouldn't dare tell you what's going through my mind, right now. Come on, let's get to the supermarket and get the things you need. Hurry, before I say something really stupid." She took his elbow. Walked quickly toward her parked car.

They did not say much as they prepared dinner. Morton could sense Colette Delaware's agitation. Several times, she had begun to say something to him, then changed her mind quickly. He waited. Helped her prepare the table. When they were seated, she looked steadily at him. Waiting for him to get her to ask her what the matter was—so she could begin.

He began to speak, and his voice was like a strong arm placed quietly around her shoulders:

"'The time has come,' the walrus said,
'To talk of many things:
Of shoes—and ships—and sealing wax—
Of cabbages—and kings—
And why the sea is boiling hot—
And whether pigs have wings.'"

"I've heard that before she said, a long time ago...don't remember where...probably in elementary school..." Colette said.

"Probably," Morton said. "It's from Lewis Carroll's *Through the Looking Glass.*

"Do you know any more?" Colette asked.

Throughout dinner, he recited verses by Lewis Carroll. Their food grew cold. She asked him to repeat the first and fourth verses from The Hunting of the Snark.

"How can you remember all these things?" she asked.

"Repetition, I suppose. I have been doing this for years," he said.

When dinner was over, she stood next to him as he rinsed the dishes in the sink. "Morton, please stay with me tonight."

"Are you sure?" he asked.

"Yes," Colette said.

"But what will the neighbors say?" he asked, and mimicked an old woman's voice: "My dear, you should have seen the line of men outside Colette Delaware's house. I tell you, I've never seen such a thing. Big, muscular, half-naked men. And we all thought she was such a Christian lady."

Colette punched his arm, "Piss on the neighbors," she said.

They drove to the hotel to collect his things.

He could see her trembling when they went into the bedroom three hours later. Neither said a word when he turned the lights off, and joined her in the bed. He turned to her, and put his arm over her; she turned on her side, away from him, and moved back to nestle into his body. She closed her eyes. Waited.

When Colette Delaware opened her eyes again, it was morning. Morton was still asleep with his back toward her. Her hand went over her body. She tried to recall sensations. Morton Dirk had not touched her. She moved closer to him, put her arms around his shoulders and fell asleep again.

The smell of coffee awoke her, and before she could get up from the bed, he came in with a tray: coffee, toast, ham and eggs, and sliced peaches.

"Wished you had given me time to fix my face. I am not at my best in the mornings. Look at you, all nice and fresh."

"Slept well?" he asked.

"Best sleep I've ever had," she said, "didn't even dream."

"Me too," Morton said. "Won't have time for lunch, though. My flight leaves at one."

"We'll have to leave by eleven. What do you want to do in the next two hours?" she asked.

"I wanted to look at your art collection. It's impressive. Jude's collection?"

"Yes, but he didn't collect them. They're all his creations," she said. "I've arranged them all from the right side of the fireplace, and around the room, back to the fireplace. Have a look, tell me if you notice something strange about them. Paintings and sculptures."

Morton walked around the room. "Some of these must be worth quite a bit. Didn't he sell his work?" Morton asked.

"Not these," Colette said, "These were all his gifts to me."

Morton stopped near the end. "They're becoming simpler," he said.

"Yes, as his drinking got worse, he tried to be more careful…and less creative. Maybe that's why he left."

"I'm very sorry, Colette," Morton said.

She avoided his eyes, looked down at the fireplace.

"I'll miss you, Morton. I'll…really, really miss you. This was the best weekend I've had since…I don't know when. Now, it's going to be very lonely. Will I see you again?" she asked.

"Ask me to see you again," Morton said.

"Please, come visit me again."

"Whenever you like, Colette."

At the airport, she tried to make lighthearted conversation, but gave up quickly. Morton held her hand until his boarding call came. She kissed him quickly on the lips, and hurried away without looking back. It was only when she was halfway home that she remembered that he had not given her his telephone number. She called directory assistance as soon as she arrived home. No, they did not have a listing for a Morton Dirk in Atlanta. She looked around the house for anything that would tell her he had been there. In the bathroom, on the bed: not a hair, not a trace No scent of him. No memory of his face. Nothing.

9

On the flight back, Morton tried several times unsuccessfully to picture in his mind the physical forces that propelled the jet, and kept aloft the heavy assemblage of metal, plastic and flesh. He tried to read from a slim volume of the Theban plays by Sophocles. That attracted the attention of the man sitting next to him. He did not want conversation. He put the book away, and closed his eyes. He saw Colette's face clearly…and heard her voice: "Please, come visit me again."

He grew angry at himself. He should have handed her the urn at the airport, and taken the next flight back to Atlanta. Instead, he had lost control. It would be dark when he arrived home. No time to decompress—to forget Colette Delaware. Tomorrow, the usual comments in class:

"Had a busy weekend, Dr. Dirk?"

"Bet he didn't sleep last night."

"Yeah, look at his eyes."

"Uh-huh, as usual."

"Got to be a woman."

"Or women."

Laughter.

And Gaynor Franklyn. Turning away when he looked at her. Unsmiling. Uninvolved. Uninterested.

The following afternoon, he hurried home when the class was over. He needed sleep desperately. At nine, he prepared for bed. At ten, the telephone rang. Telamon.

"Had a good trip to Denver?" Augustus Telamon asked.

"Very," Morton said.

"We need to talk," Telamon said.

"When?" Morton asked.

"Tomorrow evening, at the house," Telamon replied

"Tomorrow morning, at your office. Eleven thirty," Morton said.

"All right, my office."

Morton Dirk knocked on Judge Agustus Telamon's office door at eleven twenty-five the next morning. "Morning, Dad."

"Good morning, Morton. You look tired."

"Yes," Morton said, and glanced at his watch. Waited.

"How serious is your relationship with Colette Delaware?" Telamon asked.

There it was—as Morton had expected. "We've only known each other for two days," said.

"But you spent the second night of your visit to Denver at her house. She kissed you goodbye at the airport. Look Morton, every time your name, or one of the names the Organization lends you, is entered into a computer attached to a network, anywhere—except perhaps North Korea—the Organization knows. They know before I do. They know everything you do, and a lot of what you say. Any serious involvement you have with a woman poses a threat to the Organization, and consequently this places the woman at risk. You know this as well as I do."

"Does the Organization believe that celibacy will make me a more efficient employee?"

"We have never insisted on chastity for you. You are free to sleep with as many of your students in as many hotels and motels as you wish. In fact, we have ensured that you will never be surprised or disturbed. But this relationship appears to be different."

Morton's face showed no reaction to Telamon's revelation although he was surprised that they knew so much about his trysts. In that case, he could be more relaxed at his next rendezvous with Gaynor—surprise her with by going four times. He said to Judge Telamon: "Mrs. Delaware was a very pleasant and unexpected surprise. She was the first person who expected absolutely nothing from me…."

Telamon interrupted. "Morton, I…and the Organization have given you everything you have asked for, and…."

Morton continued. "Unlike you, my parents, my friends, my students, coworkers, even the poor, everyone expects something from me. For one weekend, that woman was absolutely happy because of my presence. That was a new experience for me, and I intend to repay her. I do not plan to marry or live with Colette Delaware, but I will do everything to protect…and ensure her happiness. I owe her that. I killed her husband."

"He was dying, Morton," Telamon said.

"But I stopped his heart…at a moment of my own choosing."

"So, what do you intend to do?" Telamon asked.

"I haven't thought much about it. When you called, I was angry at myself for having become sentimental over her. I do not see how she can become a threat to the Organization. She lives in Denver, for Heaven's sake."

"She is not a threat to us…yet, but she is a risk. And she may make you a threat to us. If your relationship deepens, she will inevitably find out things about you that she will not be able to accept or handle. What will you do then?"

"She will not find out about the Organization or my activities. I shall see her only occasionally, and in situations where I remain a college professor."

"It's not going to work, Morton. If you want to sleep with her, you can go to Denver every now and then and relieve your itch. But you must not become emotionally involved with Colette Delaware. It the Organization even wonders whether she is a threat, it will remove her at the earliest opportunity…no matter how much I try to protect her. Then they may wonder about you."

"They will have to kill me too, you know that. And that won't be easy."

"I know that, and thanks for the warning," Telamon said.

They looked steadily at each other. Neither blinked. The judge spoke first, "The Organization has made a suggestion. I believe it is a foolish one, but I have to give it to you: we will pay you half a million dollars if you terminate your relationship with Colette Delaware."

Morton answered almost before Telamon had finished speaking, "No."

"You're certain?"

"Yes."

"Gad, I admit that I admire you. And now I am honestly terrified. For you. You're my son, Morton. I don't want you dead."

"Then tell the Organization to stay away from Colette Delaware. If she ever becomes a risk to the Organization or to me, I shall take care of her myself. No one else must touch her. You understand that…Judge Telamon?"

"Yes. Do not make this personal, Morton. You understand our situation. We cannot continue if there is the slightest possibility of exposure of our existence."

"I have been totally loyal to the Organization. The Organization knows that."

"We know that, Morton."

"Please leave her alone, Dad," Morton said and rose. His face was drawn by a sadness Telamon had never seen before.

Augustus Telamon's frown faded slightly, appeased by the change in Morton's tone. "I'll do everything I can," he said. After Morton had left, he reached for the telephone.

"Reason for your call?" a voice answered.

"Shakespeare," Telamon said.

"King Lear?" the voice asked.

"Yes. Wait and see," he said.

"This is exceptional," the voice said.

"So is he," Telamon answered.

"Agreed. We wait and see for four months. No options."

"Accepted," Telamon said.

Later that night, Morton Dirk drove to a public telephone in a nearby mall. "Need anything?" he asked, when his call was answered.

"When?" Gaynor Franklyn asked.

"Tonight. Now."

"That's unusual, you must be really hungry."

"Bring anything?" he asked.

"Just the music. This one's on me. I think I'm hungrier. Been long enough. How far do you think you can go?"

"Four laps," he said.

"I'm game."

The next morning, Gaynor knocked on his door. Peeped in and said, "Animal."

"Come in, sit down," he said.

"No can do…sitting hurts too much. 'Bye Prof."

He called Colette Delaware on Friday night. He had at last managed to get a full night's sleep the day before.

Stood looking at the telephone for several minutes. Picked it up and dialed. It rang only once. "Hello Colette…it's Morton."

"Oh, Morton. I was sitting here hoping you would call. I miss you so much. I…. Oh, God. You didn't leave me your 'phone number. And I couldn't get if from information. And I didn't know if you'd call again."

"Colette, would you come spend a weekend with me in Atlanta?" he asked.

"Of course, Morton. Of course. Any time you want. Just a weekend though. I don't have a break in classes now. And…I wouldn't want to give you time to get tired of me."

"That will be fine," Morton said, "that will give you sufficient time to decide whether you'd spend a couple days during the Christmas break with me…in Puerto Rico."

She did not answer.

"Colette?" he asked, "Are you all right?"

He heard her sniff, and blow her nose. "What do you think? I can't talk…because I'm crying."

"Anything wrong?" he asked, knowing otherwise.

"No, idiot. I'm crying because you called. Don't you know that people cry when they're happy?"

"Did you think I wouldn't call?," he asked.

"I don't know. It was such a beautiful weekend…perhaps too beautiful to be real. But I was sitting here waiting for you to call," she said.

"I'm sorry I hadn't called earlier," he said.

"It's all right, Morton, I knew you would call…because you're a sweet guy…and I suspect you like me. I hope so, anyway."

"Two out of three," he said, "Listen, I need a hug desperately. If you're not too busy. I like to send you the ticket to Atlanta."

"Ooh, that is very generous, Morton, but I can't let you pay for the ticket. Won't be fair: I'll be the one having most of the fun."

"Please, Colette, it wouldn't be any trouble at all?"

"Don't care how rich you are Dr. Dirk, I won't let you pay for my travel and entertainment. You've already done enough. More than enough."

Morton looked at his left hand shaking from the beating of his heart. He tried to control his racing heart.

"Morton? Morton? You're there?" she called.

"I'm here. Sorry, I'm trying to adjust to an unaccustomed situation. I'm afraid you've demolished my equilibrium," Morton said.

"You're so very sweet, Morton. I really do want to see you again. By the way, may I have your 'phone number? I promise not to overdo it; but sometime, I may really want to hear your voice."

Morton read out the number for one of the two telephone lines. His stomach burned, as if he had been punched hard. The risk to her life was no longer a possibility. He just had made it likely.

"So, when can you come?" he asked. His voice forced into calm.

"Will have to call you back. Want a weekend when I don't have papers to correct. Want to just hold and look at you for two days. Won't even have to eat," Colette said.

"Don't worry, you will," he said.

She laughed. A quick whispering laugh. "I don't know how to interpret that, but I'll assume you were being decent."

"Yes, ma'am," Morton said, and, "You're very precious, Colette." He had come very close to adding: I love you, Colette Delaware.

After they had said goodbye, he went into the bathroom and looked at his face in the mirror. His eyes were red. "I'm so sorry, Colette. So very, very sorry," he said to the mirror.

The image of Letita Tsai came again—for the first time since he had met Colette. Letitia Tsai. The memory hurt like a slap: he had forgotten to tell Judge Telamon that he would never again kill a woman. And when he did, the judge would ask: "And how will you deal with Colettte Delaware if it becomes necessary?"

There was also the matter of Caraglo, and the judge's involvement in his parents' death.

He went to the telephone, and began dialing. Stopped halfway. "Damn', damn', damn'," he said, and replaced the handset. He pulled on a pair of running shoes, and jogged two miles to the shopping center. Went to a public telephone. "Need anything tonight?" he asked.

"You're all right, Morton? Something's going on with you,"

"Everything's piling up. Didn't realize how much I missed you, sometimes. Would really like to see you," he said.

"Want me to come stay with you?" Gaynor Franklyn asked.

"That wouldn't be safe for your reputation," Morton replied.

"Whatever you say. But this will cost," she said.

"Seven big ones," he said.

"Shee," she said, "For that, you can run till you die."

"Which one would you like?" he asked.

"The white and cream," she answered. "Give me an hour."

He packed a change of clothes. He'd stay at the hotel, and drive directly to Charteris in the morning. The Organization would ensure that his sleep would not be disturbed. They probably owned the bed, anyway.

The next morning, he was stiff and so sore that he checked himself carefully to see whether he was bleeding. He was not, but he soaped with great circumspection. And he had slept well: could not remember his dreams; or Gaynor leaving.

Sunday morning. He called the men's shelter to ask what was going on.

"So, how was the meeting with Jude's wife?" the superintendent asked.

"Went well. There was a small service the next day. Mostly his own family. Mrs. Delaware is a wonderful lady. Very brave," Morton said.

"Good, good. I'm glad everything's taken care of. What are you doing, now."

"Not much. Just a little TV, some reading." Morton said.

"Why don't you come on down?" the superintendent said, "Guys playing dominos and cards. Some of our volunteers will be cooking chili for dinner…again. I suppose we could always do with some more."

"Okay, I'll do a pot. See you later. What time?"

"Oh, five, six. Whatever. Better get them to eat early. Place's going to stink tonight. See you, Doc, and thanks."

The men ate at long tables. Most with heads down, not looking up unless spoken to. Most conversations hushed as if hurrying to eat before the dream ended. Sweating from the hot food and the heavy overcoats and sweaters. Ready for the cold when the dream ended. They kept their elbows away from each other: no time to start a quarrel or a conversation. A joke would be good, but who could remember anything funnier than their existences?

The man sitting on Morton's left said, "Hey, Doc, ain't never heard you say grace."

Several other men looked up: at the speaker and Dr. Morton Dirk. The murmuring and clinking of forks on china grew quieter at their table. Another came quickly to Morton's defense. "So why he got to say grace, he done the cooking and gone to the grocery."

"Ain't said nothing to you, feller. Speaking to the Doc."

Morton grinned. "I didn't hear you say grace, either. And I don't pray in public."

A man sitting directly across from Morton said, "Rich people don't believe in God." It was an accusation.

"You believe in God, Doc?" the first man asked.

"Yes, I do," Morton said.

"Leave the man alone, you fellers, you eating his food; and I ain't heard nobody saying grace to the doctor," the second man said.

"You go to church, Doc?" the first man asked again.

"Yes."

"Which church?"

Morton shrugged. "Doesn't matter." He was smiling at his interrogator.

But the man did not see the smile. Just the eyes. And in their reflection, he was alone on a dark, frigid plain; no light, but he could still see the stark landscape; and a sharp wind was tearing his clothes off. He knew he would die when his undershirt was stripped away. He shook his head. "Sorry Doc, just funning with you." He did not lift his head until he had finished eating. He left the table without looking at Morton.

"Don't know what's wrong with Jukebox this afternoon. He ain't never gone to church," the second man said. The others nodded in agreement.

Morton played dominoes for another hour. He won only one game.

"You might can cook, Prof, but you can't play dominoes for shit," one of his partners said.

"Need more practice," Morton said.

"Yeah. Come down here more often. We'll teach you to play."

"I could have whipped your butts, you guys, I only let you win because I didn't want to discourage you from wanting to play me again. Next time...." Morton said. He rose to leave.

"Listen at him. Man, we could'a beat you even if we was sleeping," one of his previous opponents said.

The men were laughing hard. "Him? Beat us? I been playing dominoes before his pa was born. We had to let you win once."

"Doc just joshing. He a nice guy."

"Ain't he though."

The only light in the parking lot came from an inadequate flood light on the adjacent side of the building that housed the men's shelter. Dark enough to make all dark colors appear black. He was walking around his car to get to the driver's side when he smelled them. Three. An ammoniacal smell of stale urine—a diabetic; fresh, and old spilled beer—Jukebox. The third wore unwashed, sweat-soaked polyester. The smells has settled around the car. They had been waiting for him. He paused, saw the faint shadow edge toward his heels. Left the key in his pocket, took his hand out slowly.

"What's up, man?" a voice behind him asked.

"Nothing. Going home," Morton replied.

"Looks like you going to have some company tonight. We coming home with you."

"You guys know this isn't going to work. Look, if you need money, I got fifty dollars in my wallet. I can get you some more at a cash machine, and we can forget the whole thing. I don't like trouble."

"You right about the fifty dollars," Jukebox said. We gonna want a whole lot more."

The man holding the gun pushed the barrel between Morton's shoulder blades. "We going for a ride, Doc. Nothing stupid. I used this thing before. Make a big, big hole in your back if you misbehave. Now, get in the car. Sunglass, you in front. Jukebox, in the back, right side. Let's go Professor Doctor."

"Where?" Morton asked, as he drove out of the parking lot. He headed for Ponce de Leon Avenue. Turned west.

"'ATM…ATM.' Like the little boy say on television," said the gunman. You gonna give Sunglass the card and the code, and everybody gonna be happy. Then we take you home…" he began to sing, "…where the buffalo roam, and the deer and the antelope play."

The other two men were laughing hard. Jukebox repeated, "Where the buffalo roam. Shit, Bazooka, you too damn' funny."

"Sunglass, take the wallet from his pocket," Bazooka said.

Morton slid forward to let the other slip his hand around to his left hip pocket.

"Good boy, good boy," Sunglass said. "Got it, Baz'."

"Now, let's see. We don't want to go to some place with too many people. Sunglass, you don't look like you could have an ATM card."

"And they take your picture when you take money," Jukebox said.

"Forgot that shit. Yeah. You got money in your house, Doc?" Jukebox asked.

"Nine hundred dollars."

"Got a computer and stuff?"

"Yes, I have a computer and some jewelry," Morton replied.

"You taking this well, Doc. Smart man. If youd'a tried anything, I would'a wasted your ass in the car."

"He ain't kidding," Jukebox assured Morton. "And this time you ain't gonna put these eyes on me. Mother's got devil's eyes," he told his companions.

"Look, guys," Morton said. "Let's get this over, now. I take you to an ATM and withdraw my maximum—eight hundred dollars. You take the money and leave me alone. I forget the whole thing. Okay?"

"Not okay, Doc. We ain't going to no ATM. You'd do some shit on us. You taking us home. I want to sleep on some nice clean sheets tonight. How many rooms you got, Doc?" Bazooka asked.

"Two bedrooms," Morton said.

"We can use that," Jukebox said. "Sunglass, you the youngest. You sleep in the living room. We gonna have a good time tonight."

"Three hundred, each," Sunglass said.

"Where you live, Doc?" Bazooka asked.

"Near Six Flags," Morton said.

"Nice house?"

"Paid one hundred and fifty thousand for it, couple years ago."

"Woo-wee," Sunglass said. I don't mind sleeping in the living room. TV and all to watch."

"You got food in the house?" Sunglass asked.

"Yes, the 'fridge is full," Morton answered.

"All right! Let's go Doc. You know the way," Bazooka said.

Morton continued to Highway 75/85. Drove south to Highway 20. Turned east.

"Know something, Doc?" Bazooka asked, "I think you using this college professor shit to hide something. You see, I used to be a cop before things went a little wrong, and they kicked my ass out. Now you, you're different from the other guys who come to do all this charity stuff at the shelter. They come in there smiling and joking like we their friends, but you can still see they're afraid. Scared to hell of us. Always waiting for one us to lose it, and pull out a gun or something. But you, you ain't afraid of nobody. Eyes remain cold…nothing make you nervous, or make you sweat. I've seen guys like you…kill a man without even thinking, like they just wiped their ass after a good shit. Maybe you teach stuff, but you something else. And I been asking myself ever since the first time I saw you at the shelter: who and what is this guy? You ain't no professor, Professor. Now, tell us, what is it you do for real?"

"No shit," Sunglass said, "Man, I never knew you was a cop, Baz. Why they throw your ass out?"

"Shut up," Bazooka replied, "I'm talking to the man, here."

Sunglass reached to pat Dirk on the shoulder. "Don't worry about Bazooka, Doc, I'm gonna take care of you…you're my friend." He pulled his hand back suddenly. "Shit, Doc, you got a fever? Man's burning up, Baz."

"He can take some aspirin when we get to his house. How far you got to go, Doc?" Jukebox said.

"Thirty minutes," Morton answered. He kept his speed just under sixty. Twenty five minutes later, they could see the lights of the Six Flags amusement park. Just two miles ahead was a newly paved road leading to a self-service storage lot. Two minutes later, "This is my road," Morton said. He was altering the circulation of blood to flood his muscles and brain, raising the temperature of his legs and arms. His abdominal muscles tightened to pump more blood from his internal organs. He inhaled deeply to satisfy his body's increased demand for oxygen, but slowly to keep his breathing quiet

"Going home," Jukebox said, "going home."

The car slowed, and turned right off the highway, speeded up again.

"Don't see no lights," Bazooka said, before Morton's right elbow crashed into his right eye. Even before the pain had registered, Morton had spun around, and grabbed his head. The snap of his neck breaking sounded like a brief handclap. The gun fell to the floor, and Jukebox lunged for it. His face met the heel of Morton's onrushing left hand. Splinters of his nasal bones tore through the base of his skull, shredding the frontal lobes of his brain.

Sunglass was trying to push himself through the door, his eyes wide in terror, hands scrabbling too frantically to find the door handle. "Oh, God. No. Please, please, please!"

"Give me my ATM card," Morton said.

Sunglass handed over the card quickly.

"Close your eyes," Morton said.

Sunglass squeezed his eyes shut. Did not see or feel the blow that crushed the left side of his head.

Morton turned out the lights, and got out to pull the three dead bodies out of the car. Took his wallet from Bazooka's front pocket. Rolled the bodies down a ditch. Looked around. No lights, or sounds of movement.

He got back into the car, and drove further on until the road widened enough for him to turn around. He drove back to the highway and turned east on the I-20. Maintained a constant speed of sixty. Remembered the story that Georgia Enoch had told him in Boston: how she had got lost in New York, been raped in her car, and how she had shot the rapist. It would amuse her to hear his own adventure. Someday, he would ask Telamon about her. Let the bastard pretend not to know her.

When he arrived home, he used a sponge and diluted Clorox bleach to wipe everything in the house that he had touched since arriving. He returned to the car with the vacuum cleaner and went over every inch of the interior. He wiped the door handle, seats, gear shift, headlamp switch, turn indicator, and steering wheel, with the sponge and bleach solution; then left the windows down to let the smell of chlorine escape. He returned to the bathroom to scrub himself thoroughly, and to spit out the memory of the three highjackers, the shelter and its occupants and its smells.

He went to bed with his mind focused on the subterranean tumult of boiling rock beneath the Himalayas, as the Indian subcontinent rammed itself further into the belly of the Asian land mass. Wondered what would happen when the weight of the Himalayas became too great for the crust to bear.

Two days later, the shelter superintendent telephoned him at Charteris College. "Hear about Jukebox and a couple of his friends?"

"No," Morton said. "They're in trouble?"

"Permanent type. Three of them found dead near Six Flags. Had a gun with them. Looks like they tackled the wrong person.... You know karate, Doc?"

"Enough to stop my girlfriend beating me up," Morton said.

"Know you had a little run in with Jukebox, but this don't make sense. Police been here asking questions. Nobody had anything to say."

"Want me to talk to the police?" Morton asked.

"Nah. Don't bother yourself. Won't help. That's how it is with these guys. See you soon."

"Thanks for letting me know," Morton said.

"Thanks for the help," the superintendent said.

The following Saturday morning, he drove to the Home Depot store three miles away for four flats of pansies, fertilizer, and pine bark chips. He spent the afternoon pulling up browning stalks of petunias and raking the old mulch to one side. Then he began turning the soil with a hand fork, digging in a fine layer of fertilizer. Straightened and stretched to ease the cramp in his back; then knelt, and started putting in the pansies. Tried to squash, but missed two plant hoppers, blue with red stripes, that jumped from the seedlings.

He spread the old mulch among the new plants, and was adding the new chips, when the voice behind him said: "When you're finished, can you do mine?" Same old joke, every time he worked in the garden.

He looked over his shoulder at his neighbor. "Sure, soon as I'm done here." Same old answer. He smiled at the thought of saying: Why don't you come up with something different, or keep your sorry ass out of my garden? Wasn't worth it—creating an enemy. Smile pleasantly, repeat the inanities. Love your neighbor.

"Had ladybirds all over my house this summer," the neighbor said.

"Yes, had to clean out the light fixtures other weekend. Must have been the aphids that brought them. There were lots on the roses" Morton said.

"Little orange buggers with black spots. They bite too," the neighbor said.

"Hadn't noticed," Morton said.

"Yeah, especially when you're sweating. Guess sweat taste like gravy to them," the neighbor said.

Morton agreed. "That's funny."

"New neighbor been asking about you," the man said. "Lady who moved in a couple months ago—down the hill. Drives a green Mercedes."

"What did she ask?"

"Wanted to know if you were married. Wife said she didn't think so. She's got a boy though, fifteen…sixteen. She's probably divorced. Never seen a husband," the neighbor said.

"My fiancée's coming to visit in a couple weeks. Don't think that would be a good time to become interested," Morton said.

"Fiancée?" the neighbor asked. He wanted to hurry back and confirm what he had always insisted to his wife: Dr. Dirk was not gay. "Better start doing something myself," the neighbor said, and walked away.

"See you," Morton said to the man's back.

Three weeks later, Morton stood at a United Airline's Gate waiting. He could have lowered his heart rate, but he enjoyed the uncontrolled pounding that shook his head and chest.

Colette Delaware had dressed to make a good impression—in black and purple, with a choker of black pearls: She succeeded. On Morton, and on a male passenger who hurried to keep up with her.

She held Morton tightly. "Hello, darling." The first time a woman had said this to him. She pressed her cheek against his. His hands and face had warmed until they were burning. "Ooh, you're nice and warm," she said.

"Good flight?" he asked.

"Very, but I was so impatient to get here and see you again. Man sitting next to me was about to ask me to marry him, I think. Gave me his card and home number. Said I could call anytime, day or night. Think I should call?" She showed him the card, and crumpled it.

"Jezebel," Morton said.

"Yeah," she answered. "Glad to see me?"

"No. But I'm a good actor," he said.

"Don't care, just grab hold of me for a couple of days. I missed you so much, Morton."

"Considering how little we know each other," he said.

"Strange, isn't it? But I try not to think of that too much. I want to enjoy it while it lasts," Colette said.

"Why? You plan to use me then dump me?"

"No, Morton," she said, "but you're too good to be real. I keep wondering whether there's a reality about you that's very different from what I know. You're so controlled. I wish I could read your mind…on the other hand, perhaps not. So, I'm just going to have a real nice weekend. I'm going to sit and stare at you all day."

"What you know of me is everything. I'm not a very exciting or mysterious person."

"Know the strangest thing about you?" she asked.

"What?"

"I forget your face as soon as I look away. Can never remember it. Got to take a photo while I'm here."

"I'll send you a good one," Morton said.

"Unh-unh. I'll take my own. Now, hold my hand. Tight. Let's pretend we're lovers."

"Are you worried about staying at my place? Strange person that I am?" he asked.

"Just try and keep me out," she answered.

"Never knew how embarrassing it could be walking with the world's most beautiful woman down an endless airport concourse," he said. "People are tripping all over themselves looking at you."

"I could always kiss you all the way out," she said.

"They'd resent that. Wasting yourself on a nobody."

"But my very own nobody. Morton? Do you think I'm presumptuous, treating you like my boyfriend?" Colette asked.

"As long as you mean it," he said.

"You're such a doll." She held his hand more tightly. "Going to have such a good time," she said.

Morton's eyes swept the crowds. Looking for other eyes that followed them. Knowing they were there—observing every detail. Knowing he would never spot the Organization's people. Could be the cleaner sifting the sand in the ashtray; or the driver of the electric car; or the airline pilot approaching. Or the lady who checked Colette's luggage tag. Or even his neighbor's wife. It didn't matter, really. Colette Delaware would be as safe as the President's wife—for the weekend.

The surveillance of the neighbor's wife verified what Morton had said to her husband: She glimpsed the back of a woman's head in Morton's blue-gray Volvo 760 Turbo station wagon before the garage door closed.

Colette's first words when she entered the house were, "This is the neatest home I have ever seen...almost too neat. Guess you don't have too many wild parties here."

"Cleaned up because you were coming," Morton said.

"Liar. The house is you. Everything under control. Everything in its place." She walked through the kitchen, entered the living room. "My goodness, books up to the ceiling." Saw the glass-fronted cabinet with the shell, rock, and fossil collections. "Interested in geology, Morton?" she asked.

"Fascinates me," Morton said. "Ever since I was a kid, and read about the movement of tectonic plates under the earth's surface. Makes you wonder how people can believe they own pieces of the planet...when it changing, and moving around. Imagine, buying and selling pieces of the world."

Colette Delaware was frowning, looking steadily at him.

He understood the question in her eyes. "Oops. Sorry. Drifted into the classroom for a second. Here, let me show you around. Didn't ask you before...do you want me to sleep in a separate room?"

"Just try it," she said. "You wouldn't be some sort of serial killer, would you?"

"You'll be safe," Morton said, "I've sworn never to kill another woman." Colette was looking out of the window, and did not see the tightening of his mouth.

"Good. That makes me feel much better," Colette said.

"Want to yourself comfortable? Come. Let me show you the bedroom." He brought her things into the room. "Got to tell you something, Colette, you're the first woman I'm ever had here."

"Liar," she said; her voice sharpened with irritation. "And you're also going to tell me you don't have a woman."

"Not lying…and don't have another woman," he said. Calmly, as if happy that she had broached the subject.

"So, what do you do when you want…?" she asked. "Your hand?"

He shrugged. "There are things I wouldn't ask you," he replied. "Even if I wanted to know."

"Time to change the subject," Colette said. And tried to hide her smile.

"Well then," he said, "what can I do to dissipate the cloud of suspicion fogging the room?"

"Just be nice to me while I'm here…want to go back with good feelings and no regret…for any sins I may commit. There's something about you that makes me so…horny. Shoot. Look at the stuff you have me saying."

"I won't lie to you, Colette," Morton said.

"And I believe you," she said. "Uncomfortable?"

"No, not uncomfortable…never was with you. Fascinated, and very excited," he replied. "Thought I would take you out to dinner, though. Wouldn't be fair to spend too much of your visit indoors."

"Fine, just as long as we do have time together," Colette said.

They ate at a restaurant in Buckhead. "Hear this is the place to see celebrities," Morton said.

"You don't socialize much, Morton?" she asked.

"Not really. Am very busy with my classes and reading. The men's shelter, and I do workout regularly…about two hours a day. And I try to get some travel in during vacations and holidays."

"Take a girlfriend with you?" she asked.

"No," Morton said. "Not much of a woman's man."

"But you must have had girlfriends," Colette said.

"Couple years ago…girl named Georgia…met her at University. Went out only with her. Then she disappeared. Not a word or a note. Have no idea what happened to her."

"What was her last name?"

"Enoch. Yes, Georgia Enoch. Why?"

"Nothing, just asked," Colette replied. "Miss her?"

"Used to. Then I got busy with other things," Dirk said.

"Good. I'm glad you didn't say I had taken her off your mind. Hate these clichés. Morton? Really, why did you ask me to come to Atlanta?" Colette asked.

"I thought I had things under control…until I came to Denver," he said.

"I think we should talk about something else at this point, before one of us says something too serious…or too sentimental…or whatever. Best not to know too much about somebody. I want us to have a really good weekend together. And no regrets afterwards. So, I'm going to try and make a good impression."

"Me too," said Morton.

"But not too good. Okay, lovey?"

She saw him try and repress the smile. He failed. Laughed out loud.

They drove down Peachtree Street to downtown Atlanta. Along the way, he pointed out the city's most famous cliché: 'Peachtree' everywhere. "Want to do anything else?" he asked.

"No, let's go home. Tomorrow, I'd like to go dancing…or whatever you'd like to do," she said.

When they arrived at the house, she said: "Know what I'd like?"

"What?"

"I'd like you to read to me again. Like you did in Denver. It was the most comforting thing I've ever experienced. The next day, I went to the bookstore and got the Alice in Wonderland books, but the poems didn't sound the same when I read them. It must have been your voice. Did you hypnotize me, Morton?"

"I can't do that, Colette, but remember I do teach this material, and I have to make people listen."

"So, will you read to me again?"

"I'd like that. Anything you want," he said.

Later, in bed, she held him close, kissed his neck and face. He kissed her so softly on her mouth that she was not certain that he had actually touched her. He rose to turn off the light and when he came back to bed, she put her head on his shoulder, and held his hand against her breasts. Waited for his hands to begin their search under her clothes.

He began—to speak:

"'Whoever you are holding me now in hand,
Without one thing all is useless,
I give you fair warning before you attempt me further,
I am not what you supposed, but far different.'"

The words lifted her off the bed, holding her suspended away from the feel of the clothes and sheets. Each word kissed her softly, brushed against her ears, face, breasts, belly, thighs and legs. And when he fell silent, she heard the words in her own voice, as if he had opened books long-closed inside her mind. She tried to move, but could not. More words crept over her again:

"'Or if you will, thrusting me beneath your clothing,
Where I may feel the throbs of your heart or rest upon
your hip,
Carry me when you go forth over land or sea;
For thus merely touching you is enough, is best,

And thus touching you would I silently sleep and be carried eternally.'"

Dirk waited until her breathing became rhythmic, and her expirations came as muted snores at three-second intervals. He rose carefully from the bed and opened a drawer in his night-stand. He reached in, and removed the knife that Point had given him. He pulled a chair to the bedside and sat close to Colette. The light from the one candle still burning was sufficient for him to see the tiny eye movements beneath her closed lids. He took the knife out of its sheath and placed the blade near the side of Colette's neck. He pulled away quickly as his hand trembled uncontrollably. He fought to control his breathing. If the blade had touched the skin, its weight would have been enough for the fine edge to draw blood.

His abdomen contracted violently, and Morton clasped his hand to his mouth as he rushed to the bathroom. He fell to his knees before the commode and vomited until he had emptied his stomach, and his diaphragm has stopped its spasmodic contractions. He rose and washed his face, rinsed his mouth with mouthwash, and brushed his teeth.

If the Organization decided to eliminate her, he would insist on doing it himself. Then what? Secrete her out of the country? Persuade her to go into hiding? Nothing would work: they would find her and kill her, and him too. For the first time, he faced the new and nauseating sensation of absolute defeat.

He returned to the bedside and began to speak; his voice just loud enough to reach her ears. And she heard his words in her dream, as she stood in a courtyard facing a two-tiered fountain, pouring into a semicircular basin of blue tiles decorated with white lilies. A man sat on the rim of the basin. She could not see his face, but his voice made her comfortable.

"I'm Morton's friend," he said. "And you're his new friend."

"My name is Colette," she said.

"Yes, I know. Morton has never felt this way about another woman. He worships you," the man said. He was dressed in a straw-colored linen suit, and wearing a sky-blue shirt. She could not see his feet, but knew he was wearing tan casuals—without socks. Mist from the fountain obscured his face, but he looked familiar.

The man continued: "He would give his life for you, but you know that."

"Yes," she answered confidently.

"How do you feel about him?"

"I've never felt so strongly about a man. Not even my husband when I was in love with him. But I don't know Morton. Not very well."

"That is not the most important thing. It's knowing that you have become Morton's world. There is no one else, nothing else, nowhere else."

"Who are you?" she asked.

"I'm...," the man began. Then he turned around to look at something in the fountain's basin. She moved nearer to repeat her question, then the dream was gone.

She was awake, but she kept her eyes closed, struggling to recall the dream. She felt for Morton. Turned toward him to say him he did not have to hesitate any more. She wanted him to take her clothes off and lie naked on her, and she would do anything he wanted; say anything he wanted. She opened her eyes. "Morton?"

It was light. And she could hear him moving about the kitchen. She went into the bathroom to wash the sleep out of her face, and to brush her hair back. Morton was at the stove. "Slept well?" he asked.

"Too well. What did you do to me last night? Fed me something to send me to sleep?"

"Wouldn't do that," Morton said.

"You did the same thing in Denver, remember? Put me right to sleep. How do you do that?"

"Words are powerful things, Colette, but also gentle. Ever heard of Audre Lorde?"

"No," Colette answered.

"Black writer. Taught English literature in New York. She wrote a poem called '*Coal*,' c-o-a-l. Says that some words are like snakes in her throat; and others want to explode out of her mouth. Exquisite metaphors…that's the essence of good literature…to make you wish you could use words that paint such fantastic pictures in the mind."

"I've never known anyone so obsessed with words," Colette said. "Anything you like better?"

His eyes smiled, and he opened his arms out toward her. "I love words, Colette. Each good word has its own smell and taste and form. Sometimes, I let them carry me away. I'm sorry. Still angry?"

"Not really. Wondered if you were trying to avoid any intimacy. No point trying in preserve my long-taken virginity, you know."

Morton grinned. "That must be the sweetest of admonitions," he said.

"No, really, Morton," she said. "If I were afraid of having sex with you, I wouldn't have slept in the same bed as you…twice."

Morton looked at her until she became uncomfortable. "I'm not going to rush and risk hurting the first meaningful relationship I've had with a woman," he said.

"Sorry, Morton," she said. "You are such an unusual person…I don't know what to say."

He turned off the burner under the frying pan, and came to the table. Took her hand and led her into the bedroom. Lifted her off the floor, and placed her on the bed. Lifted her as lightly as if she weighed no more than a pillow.

"What was that you read to me last night?" Collette asked, "Something about holding you, or touching you?"

"That was '*Whoever you are holding me now in hand,*' by Walt Whitman," Morton said, as he lifted her nightdress over her head. He undid the knot of his white bathrobe. He wore nothing beneath it.

She looked at his naked body for the first time. It looked and felt like carved wood. She stretched her arms out wide for him. She remembered screaming until her throat hurt—and wondering whether the neighbors could hear. Remembered whimpering helplessly. Remembered telling him to do whatever he wanted with her. She fell and rose. Twisted and arched. Laughed and cried. Put her mouth against his ears: "So good, so good." She felt him grow lighter until he was floating just above her, but still rubbing against every part of her body.

Then Morton and the entire room became a noise. He lifted himself off her one hour later. And the room was filled with the intense perfume of ylang-ylang and sandalwood from the candle.

"You're going to have to carry me the rest of the day," she said. "Or find me a wheelchair."

"Better feel better in a hurry," he said. "You have another night to go."

"My man," Colette said.

They spent the rest of the day at Stone Mountain Park, the High Museum of Art, and at the Zoo.

They were standing at the flamingos' enclosure when Morton said, "Not very red, these birds."

Colette asked him: "Did you know that flamingos' feathers are really white."

"And the red comes from the little red shrimp they eat?" Morton said.

"How'd you know that?" she asked.

"Read it somewhere. Geography and geology are favorites of mine, too. You pick up these things," Morton said. "Now, answer quickly. What color is a polar bear's skin?"

"Whi…She stopped. "No, must be something different. Black?"

"Yes, the skin's black." he said.

"I knew that," Colette said.

"Yeah, right," Morton answered.

"Meant what you said about going to Puerto Rico for Christmas?" She asked.

"Sure. Why?"

"I've never seen the ocean, Morton. This sounds silly...at my age. I haven't traveled much. Jude and I came from poor families, and we both considered traveling an unthinkable extravagance. That's maybe he wanted to go live in a city near the sea...eventually."

"All right then, it's Puerto Rico for Christmas," Morton said.

"And know what I want to see there? The marine phosphorescence."

"What's that?" Morton asked.

"Bioluminescent plankton called *Noctiluca*," she said. "They light up green when they're disturbed. Makes the water look like its on fire. Always wanted to see that. Am so excited already. Will be able to tell my students I actually saw it. And maybe we can visit the rain forest."

"Been reading up on the island?" he asked.

"Yep," Colette Delaware said.

It was dark before they had been halfway through the zoo.

"Must leave some more things to see for your future visits to Atlanta," he said.

"Mean that?" she asked.

"Yep," Morton Dirk said.

Colette insisted on cooking dinner that night: Baked flounder stuffed with crabmeat; wild rice, macaroni and cheese; and a salad flavored with olive oil and feta cheese into which she put every red and green vegetable there was in the refrigerator. Sliced fruit for dessert.

After dinner, Morton asked: "Would you do a little thing for me? Nothing kinky...little fantasy I've had."

"Oh, that'll be interesting," Colette said, "I can't imagine you being kinky. What's it?"

"I'd like to see you wearing something of mine...would make me feel I'm wrapped around you. Come."

They went into the bedroom, and Morton took a white silk shirt out of the closet. Handed it to Colette.

"Should I wear a tie too? Yes. Do you have a red tie?"

Morton found her a red wool knit tie.

Colette undressed except for her panties and put on the shirt and tie. "How's that?" she asked.

"Better than my best fantasies," he said. "Could you come and stand here...let me enjoy looking at you for a while." He sat at the edge of the bed; and she came and stood between his legs.

She placed his arms around her waist; then pulled his head against her belly. He sucked all her smells into himself. His hands moved down her back and thighs and legs; and back up again—up her front; down her sides; cupped her bottom; over every part of her—until her breathing quickened to gasps and she bent and spoke urgently into his ear. "Please, Morton. Now. Now...now...now."

Instead, he rose from the bed and knelt at her feet, kissed her toes, then the arches of her feet, her ankles, calves and knees; kissed the backs of her knees, touched the small dimples there with the tip of his tongue; licked the backs of her thighs all the way to the curves of her bottom. He made her sit on the edge of the bed, pushed her legs apart and licked the insides of both thighs until her body shook and her eyes filled with tears. "Please?" she asked. Her voice was far away and desperate—pleading. She rolled to the center of the bed and opened herself. For almost an entire minute, he knelt between her legs looking intensely at her body. Then he lifted her arms and wrapped her around himself.

Two hours later, before she fell into sleep, she swore to herself that she would be out of bed before him, and make them breakfast; but when she awoke, he was already in the kitchen, whipping eggs for an omelette.

"Would you like to do anything before we leave for the airport?" he asked, after they had eaten. "We have five hours. Want to make love again?"

"Would like to, but can't. You've torn me up. What I need is a good warm soak. Would you come and soap me?"

After her bath, she asked: "Can we go to a park for a stroll? I'd like to hold your hand in public," she said.

The sideways glances, the beginnings of words, the small frowns told him that she was searching for the right words for a question. She waited until they were on the highway, and the driving was easier.

"Morton?"

"Yes, ma'am."

"Do you see a lot of women?"

"Why?"

"The way you make love…that must have come from practice or experience. And a lot of that. I know it's not my business, but I'm a little embarrassed about being…target practice," she said.

"Truth is," Morton answered, "I was probably the oldest virgin at my highschool. In fact, I was technically a virgin until University."

"Oh, come on."

"Truth. Then I met a girl who was much more experienced that I…and liked sex. Boy, did she like it. Taught me enough. And let me try out things. That's the honest truth."

"But you must have a girlfriend in Atlanta?"

"Did," he said, then thought of how long it was since he had had a motel visit. "Until a month ago. The relationship got tired…just fizzled away."

"So, what do you do when…you want?" she asked.

"Want what?"

"Don't do that. You know exactly what I mean," she said.

"What do you do yourself in that situation?" he replied.

"None of your damn' business." She looked away, but he could see the upturned corner of her mouth.

"Same here," he said. "Bet you're blushing."

"Oh, you're a wicked, wicked man, Morton Dirk." She turned to look directly at him. "Ever messed around with your students? I'll bet there must be one or two in your class who'd offer you a bit of booty for an A."

"Perhaps, but no one has yet," he answered.

None of her questions had shaken his calm. She asked one last question. "How about me? Was I...good enough for you?"

"Let's say I'm deeply grateful for you; and at this moment, I am happier than I can remember...ever."

She did not say anymore until they had parked near Piedmont Park and walked toward the Botanical Gardens. For twenty minutes she would not let go of his hand. "Morton, you'll go on being this good to me?" she asked.

"I couldn't do otherwise, Colette. You're the best thing in my life."

Three hours later, at the airport, she rested her head on his shoulder as they sat at the departure gate. "Don't worry, I'm not going to do anything silly. Just going to kiss you goodbye on the cheek, and walk out of here like a brave girl. Tonight, in bed, I'll cry my eyes out. Okay?"

"Are you trying to make a grown man fall apart?" Morton asked.

"Don't think I'll ever see you do that, but I like the sentiment," Colette said.

"When you arrive, call to let me know that you're well. Please."

"Yes, of course," she replied.

A voice announced the first call for boarding her flight.

Then her row number. They rose, and she stretched up to kiss him on the cheek. He kissed her lightly on the mouth. Quickly. He was glad neither had said: "I love you." The Organization would have heard. She turned for a last look before she entered the jetway to the aircraft. He turned and left immediately.

When he returned home, he turned on his personal computer and logged on to the Internet. He did a search for Puerto Rico. Read several pages of information for visitors. Was still reading when the telephone rang. It was ten o'clock.

"I'm glad your weekend went well," Judge Augustus Telamon said, "I have a tough one for you. You and Point. Very serious business."

Fifty five minutes later, Colette Delaware called to say she had arrived safely. "Any thing exciting planned for the week?" she asked.

"No. Just a visit with my adopted dad. Wants me to come over for dinner and a chat."

"Miss you so much, lovey."

"Thanks for being my friend, Colette," he said.

He had experienced brief episodes of fear before: during his training with Point; in Houston when Stanza had shot at him; on a beach south of Savannah, when a target who expected him to bring a briefcase with three hundred thousand dollars had panicked and run off into the darkness. But these moments had lasted only seconds, before he let cold efficiency complete the mission. Colette Delaware's friendship terrified him. Made his stomach burn; awakened him at night, sweating; pictures in his mind of Colette Delaware with her throat slit lying next to the body of Letitia Tsai: Throat for throat. The Organization would not let the relationship continue indefinitely. They would kill her at the moment they had already decided. And there was nothing he could do to save her—not even by killing himself.

He could have prevented it: given her the dammed ashes and rushed back. Instead, he had deliberately seduced her with words; played the romantic idiot; flaunted her in full view of the Organization because she had not set a price on herself. She would not even accept an airline ticket. Had insisted on paying to bring the gift of herself to him. And had been indignant when he had hesitated to accept her body. He could hear her voice as clearly as if she were standing between his legs: "Please, Morton. Now. Now…now."

The best he could hope for was that they would do it quickly, before she could see the killer. They would probably send Point. He would ask Point to ensure that she died instantly. No warning. No pain.

Then. He would kill Point.

10

On the first night of Dirk's Christmas vacation, he met in Judge Telamon's basement with the judge, Clarence Point, and another man. There were no formal introductions, Judge Telamon merely said, "Morton Dirk…Al Queller." The men's eyes met for only a second.

The judge led them to a table covered with maps and building plans. Morton spoke to the image of Al Queller, still sharp in his memory—pale white skin, bald, gray eyes; less hair and more lines. At the earliest opportunity, I'm going to blow your head apart…two bullets…for my mother and my father…as soon as Maz Reyes is taken care of. Then he put the thought away.

"Point," the judge said, signaling at him to start.

Clarence Point kept his eyes on the judge's face as he spoke: "House is on a nine-acre wooded lot. Closest neighbor is two miles away. Out of sight behind a small rise, but within earshot of loud gunfire on a cool night. The house is surrounded by an eight-foot wire fence. Two German Shepherds have the run of the enclosure. Inside the house is a French poodle…smart and absolutely fearless…never lets Reyes out of his sight. The house has a monitored alarm system bottom and top floors. Reyes will be home with his wife, daughter, and daughter's boyfriend for the week before Christmas, and for two days after. Judge Telamon will attend dinner along with six other guests on Christmas Eve at eight p. m.. We will enter the grounds in Judge Telamon's car. I will chauffeur. Dirk, you and Queller will remain concealed in the back. You may have to wait for several hours in the car, so the windows will be cracked slightly, and there will be blankets. If necessary, you can move into the trunk from the back—backrest will not be latched. The dark windows will hide the condensation from your bodies. The dogs will be caged during the arrival and departure of the guests, and the alarm will be off. The judge will be the last to leave, having business to discuss with Reyes. I will probably be in the kitchen helping. When the judge is ready to leave I'll come to get the car. I'll drive around to the front door to meet the judge. We expect Reyes…perhaps with his wife, to see the judge out. At that moment, I shepherd Reyes back into the house. You come in then. Quickly. If something goes wrong, and you need to come in immediately, I unlock the car doors with the remote…you move in. Let me warn you about Reyes: Three of us against him just evens the odds. He's very, very good. We also have at least five other people to take care of. The only advantage we have is a few seconds of surprise. No mistakes…or we get our asses reamed. From now on, until the last minute, we rehearse everything in our minds. Over and over. And we use guns…with silencers. Can't risk getting close enough to Reyes to use a knife. We have an envelope of photographs of all the people we expect to encounter in the house…except for invitees. Look at them until you can pick them out in a crowd. Behind each photo is the name and characteristics of the subject.

"Now, we will go over the house plans until you're sure that you could find your way around in the dark. Every room, top and bottom, bathrooms, closets, pantry. Know where every piece of furniture is. Every living thing in the house dies after we get the information we need from Maz Reyes. Each one of us—Dirk, Queller and I will be responsible for two terminations…I will assign these on Christmas Eve. We take away every piece of computing equipment and software, then burn the house and contents…down to the foundation.

"The three of us will be going to have a look at the property. A driver will take us to the house, drop us off in the dark…and return to pick us up next night…morning. We observe for twenty four hours, until we know where every tree, every twig, and every rock is. Been to have a look last week…so I have a general idea of the layout." Point stopped and looked at the judge.

"That's about it. I can't think of anything you've left out," Judge Augustus Telamon said.

"Except for Plan B," Point said.

"What's Plan B?" the judge asked.

"It's unlikely that things will go exactly as I've outlined. In the event that they do not, each of us will be on his own. The important thing is that no one escapes…and we get the computer. With Maz Reyes, I suspect that we'll be using Plan B."

Over the next four nights, the men pored over the plans of the house and the grounds. Then, at two in the morning of the fifth day, they left in a van driven by one of Telamon's guards. They wore camouflage suits, and carried sixteen-gauge shot guns, hunting licences, and powerful binoculars—a hunting party. In cavities in the seat cushions were ten-millimeter pistols with attached silencers. There were backpacks containing water canteens and high-calorie biscuits. Two hours later, the driver said, "Here." He slowed down and turned off his lights. Three seconds. Time enough for Dirk, Point, and Queller to roll out and vanish silently into pines at the side of the road. The van accelerated and disappeared around the corner a few yards ahead.

"Okay, the drive to the house should be ten feet to the right," Point said and walked into the intense darkness. The others followed the faint noises of his feet on the damp leaves and pine straw. "Here we are. Downhill to the house. We stop as soon as we see lights. Wind's coming our way…dogs won't smell us this far. Should be a clump of honeysuckle coming up where we can stop and see the house. If it gives good cover, we stay there until tomorrow morning. This evening, soon as the sun sets, we circle the property. House is on the southwest slope of the hill…setting sun will be behind us. We check out any paths leading from the house. Another thing: our best plans will not take care of every contingency. With Maz Rayes, we will never have every thing covered. Next to the judge, he's the smartest man I know. Any questions?"

"No."

"No."

A few minutes later, his footsteps halted. "Here," they heard him say. "On the right…little steep."

Morton and Queller followed, hauling themselves up a slope by grabbing on to overhanging branches.

"Slowly. Plant your feet firmly. No skid marks on the ground," Point said.

"Here we are," he said a moment later. They continued toward his voice until their outstretched hands touched the vines. "Okay," he said. We rest here until it's light enough to move around. Want to pee or crap, do it upwind, bury it. Don't go far."

They sat on the ground with their backs against tree trunks. Facing downhill, where they expected the Maz Reyes's house to be, waiting for dawn.

The faint reddening of the sky showed the enormous Swiss-style chalet of sandstone and cedar that the Organization's money had afforded Captain Reyes. An hour later, a man wearing a gray tracksuit came out of an attached room, and began jogging slowly around the inner perimeter of the fence. Soon, the two German Shepherds joined him, one on either side of his ankles, moving so easily that they seemed to glide with the precision of shadows. After fifteen minutes he went back into the room. "Caretaker," Point said.

A few minutes later, a man and woman came out of a side door, and walked to the front gate. They wore black tracksuit. They spoke briefly then started off at a slow jog, following the same track as the earlier runner. The dogs soon followed. "Reyes and his daughter," Point said.

Half an hour later, the couple went inside. The caretaker returned with a large bowl of water for the dogs and a smaller dish from which he fed the animals by hand. When they had eaten, he chained them to their kennels and went inside for the poodle which he let run around the yard for an hour.

The Reyes family and their guest left in a Range Rover. "Other man's an engineer," Point said.

The caretaker appeared a couple more times to sweep the drive to the fence, and to clean the lawn with a leaf-blower.

Sometime near noon, Queller took a roll of toilet paper from his backpack, and moved silently up the hill. Morton moved closer to Point. "If you don't answer, I'll take that for a 'yes.' Is Queller the man who killed my parents?"

He looked steadily at Point. The other man's gaze did not waver from the house. Morton returned to his seat at the base of a white maple.

At four thirty, the Reyes returned and the caretaker helped them carry several grocery bags, boxes and crates into the house.

Point rose. "Time to look around. They're busy inside." The men circled the house slowly, studying every square foot of the surroundings. When they returned to the clump of honeysuckle, it was totally dark. The men waited silently for morning. Except for Morton's question, only Point had spoken during the last sixteen hours.

At three the next morning, they set off up the hill to the main road. At four o'clock precisely, the van stopped at the same point it had let them off. The lights died, and three seconds later came on again after the van had made a slow U-turn in the road. They headed south.

Morton slept in his old room at Telamon's residence. He awoke at two in the afternoon. Mrs. Mountrie cooked him a late lunch of salmon steaks, buttered mash potatoes and steamed broccoli. "Don't know what you've been doing, but looks like you need some good healthy food inside you. Judge said not to wake you up for breakfast this morning."

"Yes. Had a late night. And I'm still stiff. Anyway, I've got to rush home as soon as I've finished. Thanks, Mrs. Mountrie," Morton said.

"When you going to get some nice young woman to take care of you? Bachelorhood could make you die young, you know," Mrs. Mountrie said.

"That will be my New Year's resolution," Morton said.

"Better hurry up or I'm gonna tell my daughter about you. Second one. Pretty girl. Uh-huh, very pretty. And not the sort of girl you want to mess with."

"She must be a like you, then," Morton said.

"Oh, you got a sweet tongue in your head, Mr. Dirk," said Mrs. Mountrie. Then she frowned, not quite certain what Morton Dirk had meant.

On Christmas Eve, Augustus Telamon's house was empty except for the judge Telamon and the guards at the front and back. Morton arrived first, then Point, and a few minutes later, Queller. At six in the evening, Judge Telamon's Lincoln Town Car pulled out of his driveway, and headed toward Highway 75, North. In the darkened car, Point went over the sequence of events and possible eventualities. "If there are guests, take them out first; and the help. Take out the daughter's boyfriend. I take care of Reyes. I want the wife and daughter kept alive. If one of them pulls a gun, shoot to disarm...abdomen or shoulder. I want to use them to make Reyes talk. Torture won't work. Queller, you take care of the help and guests. Dirk, you get the daughter and wife. Everybody got that?"

"If the women are to be killed execution style, I will not do it," Morton said.

"What?" Telamon and Point asked together.

"I said: I will kill the women if they threaten any of us, but I will not serve as executioner of two helpless women,"

"Are you planning on defending them, too?" Telamon asked.

"No," Morton said, "I have no interest in the women's fate, I think I have stated my position very clearly."

"Why didn't you say this before?" Point asked.

"You hadn't told me I would be responsible for the women."

"You have any problem disarming them…if they are armed?"

"None. I will kill them if they threaten any of us."

"We better get this settled before we get to the house. Dirk, you're responsible for keeping the two women alive. We may need them to make Reyes talk. When that's taken care of, I will dispose of the women. Understood?"

"Yes," Dirk and Queller said.

"Judge?" Point asked.

"You're in charge of the operation. We do exactly as you say from this point," Judge Telamon replied.

"Good. Anything else? Anybody?"

"No," the others replied.

"Let's go over the operation again," Point said. "From arrival at the gate to departure. We leave the way we came…no rush. And keep Plan B in mind. One last thing…the wife and daughter of Maz Reyes are not helpless women."

Morton could imagine Telamon's face: eyes and lips narrowed into thin horizontal slits. There would be consequences—after the operation. He had just reduced his usefulness to the Organization. Their second confrontation with defiance: first, Captain Maz Reyes, then Dr. Morton Dirk. And Colette Delaware.

Morton forced his mind into the approaching house. Looked into the faces of the occupants; moved around to each room. Out to the grounds of the estate; past each rock, tree and slope. The pictures in his mind grew more vivid as he shunted blood from his arms and legs to his brain and internal organs. His fingers and toes turned as cold as a corpse's. He relaxed. Ready.

When they came into view of the house, Point said, "Down. Spotlights at the gate."

They heard the squeal of metal as the gates opened. Point rolled down his window six inches. "Judge Telamon," he said.

"Come on in. Park near front door." The voice was heavily accented. East European, Morton thought.

Point rolled up the window, and the car moved forward. "New face. Armed with an Uzi submachine gun. Nasty. Get into the trunk," he said. "I'm going to crack all the windows a small bit. Don't breathe too much."

The car stopped and the guard stood ten feet away from the passenger's side. He moved closer as Point held the door open for Judge Telamon, and he peered into the back. He bowed hid head toward the Judge, eyes never leaving the two men. "Good evening, sir."

"Good evening, Merry Christmas," Judge Telamon said.

"And to you too, sir. Thank you."

Point locked the door, and followed the judge to the front door. The guard tested the handles of all four doors, and looked through cupped hands into the back. The men heard his footsteps fade away, then the sound of the gate closing. Queller pushed against the rear seat and crawled forward. "Son of a bitch is leaning against the gate…might hear us if we move about too much. I'll keep an eye on him."

Morton was lying on his back with his knees drawn up, and his hands crossed on his chest; his right hand resting on the butt of the heavy pistol holstered on his left side. He closed his eyes; let his breathing become shallow. Wondered what Colette would be doing at that moment. He would call her early in the morning. Fly to Denver if he could get a flight. He had forgotten to buy her a present. He would call and decide what he should do. Perhaps book flights to Puerto Rico…if she still had time before her classes began.

Captain Maz Reyes and his wife were waiting at the front door for Judge Telamon. "Judge Telamon. Welcome, welcome. Merry Christmas. Clarence Point. Welcome. Merry Christmas. Feliz Navidad."

Reyes and his wife embraced Augustus Telamon. Shook hands with Point. Marva Reyes put her arm through the judge's, and escorted him inside. A younger couple waited in the foyer. Reyes introduced them. "My daughter, Rosario…and her fiancé, Arturo Albarrán."

"I'll go help in the kitchen," Point said.

"Ah, no. Not in the kitchen," Marva Reyes, said. "Judge Telamon, would you mind if Mr. Point ate with us? There's room at the table."

"Not at all, not at all. Point?" Judge Telamon said.

"Thank you, sir," Point said.

"Now, let's go into the living room and meet the other guests," Reyes said.

A man rose from the couch when they entered. Near seven feet tall. Green eyes, blond. Face, all vertical planes, except for the broken nose which leaned to the right, toward an ear with the top third of the lobe missing, as if it had been sheared off with a razor. He wore a black suit, pearl grey shirt and matching tie.

The woman looked like the late diva Maria Callas. Her skin was pale flawless white, and her intensely black hair hung past her shoulders. Her eyes were purple. She wore a long crimson dress clearly fashioned to draw stares.

He leaned toward Telamon, bowed slightly from the waist and extended his hand.

"Judge Augustus Telamon…Petros Smetuc," Reyes said. "And his wife, Gerta. From Yugoslavia. Petros is a wine importer. We'll be enjoying some of his cellar, tonight."

Smetuc bowed again.

"Wonderful," Telamon said.

Reyes introduced Point.

Smetuc's mouth twitched at one corner. Telamon assumed that the other wanted to speak. He smiled at Smetuc.

"Captain Reyes speaks very enthusiastically of you. He jokes that when he grows up, he wants to be like you."

Judge Telamon laughed. "Maz is a flatterer. And one with unparalleled skill. Careful, Mr. Smetuc. You may find yourself doing him a favor…and thanking him for the opportunity."

"Yes, yes," Smetuc continued. "I know him well…almost as well as he knows my wine. Fortunately for us, Marva keeps him disciplined. Eh, Marva?"

Marva Reyes smiled. A wide, Christmas Eve smile meant for everyone. "Should we have the sherry, caro?" she asked her husband.

"Sherry, everyone?" Reyes looked around. They all nodded, except for Rosario Reyes. She had left the room. Point caught Telamon's eyes. Looked to the left. The judge turned to his right and moved closer to admire a painting of a cluster of huts on a steep hillside. Noticed the daughter's absence. Reyes rang a silver bell and almost immediately, the caretaker and his wife came in with a tray of carved crystal glasses, and another with two wine bottles.

They put the trays down on an ornate mahogany cabinet and began pouring the wine.

The daughter was still missing when, Reyes lifted his glass for a toast.

"Shouldn't we wait for Rosario?" Telamon asked. Saw the quick glance between Reyes and his wife.

"Querido," she said to Arturo Albarrán, "Could you go find Rosario. Didn't know where she could have gone to."

The couple came back within a minute. Rosario's face was slightly flushed. "So sorry," she said. "Didn't think anyone would miss me for a few seconds."

"Papá is about to make the toast," Marva Reyes said.

Captain Maz Reyes lifted his glass. "To Judge Augustus Telamon, and my dear old friend Clarence Point; to special new friends, Petros and Gerta Smetuc; to my daughter and her fiance Arturo, a wonderful young man…A very merry Christmas. I am sincerely honored that you have blessed our house with your presence and friendship on this special night."

They raised their glasses. Point wondered what Rosario had left outside the doorway to the foyer when her shadow had bent toward the wall. The young couple remained near the door.

Fifteen minutes later, the caretaker's wife appeared at the archway between the living and dining rooms, and bowed toward Marva Reyes.

"Dinner is served," Marva said.

"Liria has prepared a stuffed roasted goose," Maz Reyes said. "And an array of Cuban dishes and sweets. We will be eating for hours, I promise you."

Reyes sat at the head of the long mahogany table. Judge Telamon sat at his right, and anticlockwise around the table were Smetuc, Gerta, Marva, Arturo, Point, and Rosario.

Point smiled his faint wry smile. Cooked goose. Your goose is cooked, Captain Reyes. Then he stopped smiling. Looked at the face of his host. Maz Reyes was laughing loudly at something that Smetuc had said. Perhaps they were laughing too…about the goose. Only it Telaman's goose that was cooked. And his too. He lowered his hands to smooth the napkin on his knees. Felt the car's remote control in his pocket; moved it so he knew exactly where the door-opener button was.

The food was exquisite. Telamon wondered how Reyes and his family managed not to surrender to their cook's accomplishments. Now, there was a woman who could match Mrs. Mountrie…except perhaps at making bread pudding. Until he ate Liria's flan. "Did your cook fall from heaven," he asked Reyes.

The captain roared. "Hear that. Marva? Judge Telamon asked if Liria fell from heaven," he repeated; although everyone had heard Telamon.

"We must watch our guests, Judge Telamon," Marva said. "Otherwise they'd be in the kitchen trying to offer her great amounts of money to leave us."

"And who could blame them. The lady is a treasure," Telamon said.

Petros Smetuc joined in, loudly, ensuring that everyone heard him too: "Like the great cook, Anatole, in the books by the English writer,

Wodehouse. Yes, P. G. Wodehouse. Very funny. Always somebody with great intrigue trying to steal Anatole away from his employer."

The others nodded in agreement. Yes, that was also amusing.

Dinner continued for an hour and a half. Finally, Reyes dabbed his lips with his napkin, and placed it on the table. "I know it is agony to rise from the table, but we must allow Liria and her husband to clear the table. Please, let us go into the living room." He led the way into the adjoining room.

Arturo and Rosario remained behind to help with the cleaning up. Telamon signaled for Point to sit opposite him, near the door. They sat in a rough circle about the room. Point adjusted the remote control in his pocket again.

Captain Reyes went to the liquor cabinet and came back with a bottle of Chartreuse liqueur. "Green, for the season," he said. "A drop for everybody?"

No one protested. Point took a small sip from his glass, rested it on a nearby table. He did not like the heavy feeling in his head. Too much to eat and drink, although he had had less than the others, especially Reyes. But that would not matter. He had seen Reyes remain lethal when another man would have required hospitalization.

Then Reyes suddenly became serious. "Judge Telamon, I asked my friend Petros Smetuc to dine with us tonight because I wanted him to introduce you to an opportunity for expansion in Eastern Europe.

Judge Telamon appeared incredulous. "Expansion? Expansion of what into Eastern Europe?"

"Of the Organization, Judge. We can speak freely here. Nothing anyone says will leave this room."

"This is not the time and place to discuss business, I don't think, Maz. If Mr. Smetuc wants to discuss a business proposition, we can discuss it in more appropriate circumstances. And I'm not sure what Organization you have in mind."

"Our Organization, Judge Telamon," Reyes repeated. His eyes had narrowed and his face was pale—almost as white as the napkin he had wiped his mouth with.

Point's lethargy vanished. He placed both hands on his laps. Leaned forward. Rosario and her fiance had not come back into the room.

Smetuc cleared his throat. "An association would be very lucrative, Judge Telamon. The leadership and financial support we are starving for, could return billions into your organization within ten years."

"Thank you for your confidence Mr. Smetuc, and I think you have been misinformed about my capabilities. But I would like to hear some more about your proposition, although I must warn you that it seems much too ambitious for me. Again, I am not comfortable discussing these matters after a Christmas Eve dinner. You understand?"

"Yes, yes. Quite," Petros Smetuc said. His eyes said otherwise.

"Well, can we change the subject to something more in keeping with the occasion?" Telamon asked. " A toast of thanks for an incomparable dinner?"

"Hear, hear," Smetuc said.

Reyes joined the toast. "To special occasions," he said, "like this one." His eyes met Point's. "Clarence, would you please remove your gun slowly, and put it on the coffee table? Slowly. Rosario and Arturo both have sixteen-gauge shotguns pointed at you. They're excellent skeet shooters."

Point unbuttoned his jacket and opened it wide so that the butt of his gun was visible. He gripped the end of the butt, keeping his fingers away from the trigger guard. Pulled the gun from its holster and carried it to the coffee table.

"Lift your pants," Reyes said.

Point pulled his pant legs above his ankles. No ankle holster. He drew his hands back up along his legs. Pressed the button on the remote control with his thumb when his hand slid past the box.

"Good," Reyes said. "I'm afraid I must impose the same indignity of you, Judge Telamon. I know you do not carry a weapon, but one should never assume. Petros...would you?"

Smetuc ran his hand over the judge. Telamon said nothing. And Reyes did not have to explain further. The judge's refusal of Smetuc and Reyes's offer was a death sentence for all of them. The best chance of survival was the window of a few hours they would have by killing Augustus Telamon and Clarence Point. A few hours before the Organization detected trouble. Perhaps just enough time for them to be airborne—heading for Paraguay. A longer interval before the Organization located them. Then, to Brazil. Bigger place. More difficult to find nondescript Venezuelan immigrants there.

The locks on Judge Telamon's car clicked open. The guard heard the noise and looked toward the house, expecting to see the guests leaving. He raised his machine pistol to waist level, and his right index finger curled around the trigger. He walked to the car, keeping it between him and the house. He had just recognized the small steel circle above the descending window of the car as the cylinder of a gun silencer, when it coughed, and recoiled slightly. A dark spot appeared in the center of the guard's forehead.

"Not bad," Queller said to Morton as they raced toward the house.

In the living room of the house, Reyes walked toward the gun on the table. "Sorry...Judge, Point."

Rosario and Arturo came into the room with short-barreled shot guns leveled at Telamon and Point. Their hands did not shake.

Smetuc took his wife's elbow. "Nothing more for us to do here," he said. They walked into the hallway.

Reyes picked up Point's gun. Looked at his wife, and tilted his head toward the doorway. "You and Rosario, go upstairs and get ready. Arturo and I can take care of things here."

He aimed the pistol at Point's head.

Dirk and Queller stood back from the bay window of the dining room. "Got to take a chance through the glass. Hope it's not double-paned. You take out Reyes, I'll go for the other guy. May have to fire twice, quickly, in case the first shot is deflected. Ready? Now!"

One bullet hit Arturo Albarrán in the right shoulder, and knocked him to the left. The shotgun fell from his hands. Before he could regain his balance, the back of his head exploded, sending shards of bone into the ceiling.

At the same instant, another bullet tore away Maz Reyes's chin. The gun in his hand wavered for an instant, and Point dove to his right, knocking Telamon to the floor. Reyes fired at his rolling body, and Point felt a flame lance through his right side. A second bullet cut a furrow through his collar before Morton's second bullet punched Reyes in the chest. Before he hit the ground, a third bullet entered Reyes's head just above his right ear.

"Kitchen," Morton said, and the men ran to the side of the house. They saw the backs of the caretaker and his wife as the couple ran toward the noise in the dining room. Queller kicked the door open. The caretaker spun around and Morton's bullet tore into his heart, throwing him against the counter. The cook ran back into the kitchen and saw her husband body twitching on the floor. Her lips drew back in snarl and she leaped toward a cleaver lying near the sink. Queller's bullet hit her between the eyes, just as her finger touched the riveted handle of the cleaver. Her body arched backward in the beginning of a failed twisting reverse somersault.

A woman was screaming in Spanish from upstairs. Marva Reyes. "Maz! Maz! What's going on down there?" Her footsteps started on the stairs. Stopped.

Silence.

Queller and Morton edged toward the door. The light from the ceiling sent their shadow out of the kitchen into the hallway. The light switch was near the door. Morton turned around and shot out the paired fluorescent bulbs. Queller looked quickly around the door jamb and pulled back quickly. Shotgun pellets tore away several inches of the wood frame where his face had been. Morton moved closer. Queller straightened up. "Going to take a running jump across the hallway into the dining room. Think you can distract the shooter? Throw a pan around the door?"

Morton nodded, took a large sauté pan from a hook over the sink. "Ready."

Queller took a few steps back and ran toward the door. His threw his hands back as his left leg braced for the jump. Morton threw the pan around the doorway and stuck out his leg just as Queller leaped into the air. Queller's body tumbled into the hallway and the shotgun roared twice, kicking the gunman's body halfway back into the kitchen. "For my parents," Morton said silently as he leaped into the hallway, twisting his body to the left as he sailed through the air. Rosario Reyes had pulled the shotgun pump halfway back when the first bullet hit her in her left breast. She fell forward down the stairs, and a second bullet went through the top of her head and into her neck.

Morton ran into the dining room. Point was leaning against the dining room table with his left hand pressed against his side. His gun pointed at Morton's head. Point lowered the gun. "Queller?" he asked.

"Hit. Daughter got him when we tried to get out of the kitchen. I got her. Cook and other man dead. Guard dead."

"Damn'. Damn'. Damn'." Telamon said. He was shaking in fury. "Three left…upstairs. Wife and Smetucs. We'll have to try and get the wife alive. Only chance of getting any information. Point? How are you?"

"Nothing lethal," Point said.

"Can you walk?" Morton asked.

"Sure. Can't run, though."

"I'm going upstairs," Morton said. He picked up Albarrán's shotgun. "Can you cover me with this?"

"Yes," Point said. He holstered his handgun, and took the shotgun.

"What do you want me to do?" Telamon asked.

"Stay out of the way," Point said. "Ready?" he asked Morton.

"When you are," Morton replied.

Point inserted the barrel out of the hallway and angled it upwards toward the top of the stairs. There was sharp report from upstairs and a hole appeared in the floor in the middle of the doorway. Point fired twice, and Morton launched himself out and up the stairs. His bullet tore along the flexor muscles of Marva Reyes's right arm. The gun fell to the second step. She knelt and reached for it with her left hand. Morton's hand grabbed her wrist and he pulled hard. The woman fell headlong down the stairs toward him. Her fingers reached for his genitals, and he struck down sharply on her hand with the butt of his gun. She continued tumbling down the stairs.

Morton ran toward the guest room. Empty. No sound. He fired through the door of the walk-in closet then kicked the door open. Not enough clothes to hide anyone. He went back into the master bedroom, kicked the door open and dove in, rolled on the floor, his gun sweeping around. He fired into the clothes cupboard again and into the bathroom. Empty. He looked into the other two bedrooms then went to the window at the end of the hallway. It was closed but unlocked. He lifted it and looked out. Smetuc was on the other side of the fence helping his wife climb down. Morton changed the magazine in his gun and slipped it back into its holster. He crawled through the window, slid down the roof to the garage roof, then turned around to lower himself to the ground. The gutter rang out near his hand, and flecks of paint and metal stung his face as a bullet penetrated it two inches away from his face. A second and third bullet hit the garage door as he fell to the ground. He fired at a dim shape disappearing into the woods, and he ran for the fence. Scrambled over the top and ran toward the spot where he had last seen movement. He lay on the ground to catch his breath and to consider the Smetucs possible moves. Directly ahead was small gully running north to south across the estate. North, it pointed uphill toward the drive to the highway. South, it ran steeply down hill to the nearest neighbor's backyard. Morton hurried toward the depression. He could move quickly because he knew where every obstacle lay. At the bottom of the gully, he paused and sniffed the air. Walked uphill and took quick shallow breaths. Turned and walked in a circle in the other direction and did the same. Perfume—downhill.

He climbed up the steep bank. It would be easier moving along the top of the gully—fewer boulders and fallen logs. The scent of Gerta's perfume grew stronger. Then he could hear them. He quickened his steps until he could hear their labored breathing. They were twenty feet away. Too dark to see. Then ten feet. He could distinguish between them now. Man on left, heavier breathing. Woman closer. Morton reached for a three-inch flashlight in his pocket. Turned it on and flung it into the gully. The pencil of light gave just enough illumination for him to see the shape of Smetuc looking in the opposite direction, the pistol in his hand searching frantically. Morton fired twice into his back. Gerta's mouth opened wide to scream. Morton aimed at her chest, then at her head. As she collapsed to the ground, he heard her say, "Aaah." As if she had finally understood the hopelessness of her predicament. Morton climbed down to retrieve his flashlight, then turned back to the house.

He was irritated. Had been forced to kill two women. The Organization had won again.

Point was downstairs sitting opposite Marva Reyes. There was saliva dripping down her chin and down the front of her dress. Her torn right arm lay across her thighs and she pressed a cushion against it.

"Judge's upstairs searching. Go check on him," Point said.

Morton went upstairs, toward the noise in the master bedroom. Telamon was in an adjoining room. "Got the computer, here, and all the diskettes I could find. Help me carry this stuff to the car."

Morton helped him load the car: One desktop and two laptop computers. A briefcase of diskettes.

Telamon went into the living room. "Mrs. Reyes, where are the diskettes with information on your husbands in Miami and Europe?"

The woman spat at him. "Kiss my ass," she said.

Telamon shrugged his shoulders. "Can't waste any more time asking you questions, Mrs. Reyes. But we will get the information out of you. I promise you it will be very painful."

She spat at him again.

Point looked at her dress: tight at her bosom with long folds of brilliant red and orange silk down to her feet. Marva Reyes seldom hid her superb figure—especially in the company of men. "I know where the diskettes are, sir," he said.

"All right then, finish it," the judge said.

Point raised his gun and fired. The bullet pierced her heart. Marva Reyes fell forward, her eyes fixed on Telamon. She spat again. "Both of you," she said.

Point said to Morton, "Look in her panties."

"What?"

"In her panties. I just remembered something Maz said once: 'A woman's got the safest pockets.'"

Morton lifted the dead woman's dress and pulled down her hose and panties. Two diskettes were taped to her lower abdomen, just above her pubis.

"Let's go," Telamon said.

Morton helped Telamon carry four incendiary devices back to the house. Point told him how to set their timers. One hour later, the windows of the house shone a brilliant orange before they shattered to air in to feed the fire's demand. It roared as it jumped towards the roof, licking at the ceilings and sending fingers and tongues of flame outside to explore and devour the eaves and the cedar shingles.

11

Jeanette Cotton frowned at Colette Delaware. She was incredulous. "You slept with the man who brought your husband's ashes to Denver, the day after you met him?"

"No, I didn't actually sleep with him. We only slept in the same bed, but we didn't have sex or anything…not even a kiss…just touched," Colette replied.

"And then…you went and spent a weekend with him in Atlanta. At his home. Alone. And you still didn't have sex?" her best friend continued.

"Not the first night. Next day, I couldn't take it any more…I almost had to make him," Colette said.

"So, the man lay next to you, on two nights, and didn't try to get into your pants? What kind of story is that, Colette? Is the guy for real, or you're putting me on?" Jeanette asked. "Is the guy some kind of freak?"

"We did it the second day, and the night after…about six times. I don't remember how many times…but I remember I was in pain for about two days."

"Girl, you so full of it. First, the guy won't touch you, then he can't stop once he starts. This is some frightening shit. You're sure the guy isn't some kind of pervert. How do you know you didn't get yourself involved with some criminal?" Jeanette asked. "Let me see his picture. You got one?"

"Shoot. I forgot again," Colette said. "And I had brought my camera. Didn't take a single picture. But I had such a nice time in Atlanta. Morton's a really sweet man, Jeanette. You know how good it feels when you like somebody so much, you feel that you could walk on water for them? Well, he makes you feel that he would walk on water for you. I've never felt that good with any man before…not even with Jude when I first met him. And he's so smart. Morton's not a criminal, Jeanette. Criminals don't spend their lives teaching poetry and writing at a University."

"You're sure he ain't into drugs or something?" Jeanette asked. "Maybe the man's some kind of weird confidence man. You know like…treats you like royalty…drives you crazy in bed…. Next thing, borrows your credit card. Wouldn't be surprised if somebody told me he was some kind of serial rapist. There are a lot of guys like that around, you know. There was a story in the paper the other day about this guy who screwed a bunch of women out of their money…told them he was a doctor…had a stethoscope and everything. I'll bet…."

"Jeanette?" Colette said.

"Yes?"

"Can you hear the crap coming out of your stupid mouth, girl?"

"Sorry. I was just worrying about you. But what if he's in some kind of illegal stuff?" Jeanette asked.

"I don't think he'd tell me that, but the guy drives a Volvo station wagon, for heaven's sake. No expensive jewelry or flashy clothes. But his clothes are classy, though. Only Joseph Aboud suits, and Johnson and Murphy shoes. Basic colors."

"I don't know," Jeanette Cotton said. "Something's not all there. Can't think what it is. Maybe it's you. So tight with your legs since Jude left. Suddenly, you can't keep them closed. Maybe you just stayed too long without."

"Shut up, Jeanette. How do you know so much about my sex life?" Colette asked.

"From you," Jeanette answered.

"I don't know what to do," Colette said. "When I'm away from Morton, I'm not sure how I feel about him. But when I'm with the man, I'm jelly. It's not his looks...he's sort of ordinary looking. It's his voice. As soon as that man opens his mouth, or says something in my ear, I want to tear my clothes off, and pull his whole body inside me. And you should see that body...not an ounce of fat. Just muscle...hard, hard muscle. And you know what his house is filled with?"

"Condoms, probably."

"Sometimes you piss me off, you know. I'm serious now. His house is filled with books. Books, you hear, good books. Not all the inspirational crap you buy and don't read."

"Okay, okay. I believe you. I just want to see him next time he's in Denver. Okay?" Jeanette Cotton said.

"Sure," Colette Delaware said.

"So. When's he coming back to Denver?"

"Said he'd try to come spend Christmas with me," Colette said.

"Try and come? Won't he be on vacation? You told me he taught at University," Jeanette said.

"Yes, but he has to help his adoptive father with some family business. Looks like the father is loaded."

"That's what he told you."

"No, Jeanette. I've been to Morton's house. You can tell when people are seriously rich. Not a cheap thing in the house. And nothing flashy."

"I don't know, girl. Maybe I'm just a little jealous. Me with a husband who don't even know there's a dishwasher in the house."

But Colette remained worried. On her flight back from Atlanta, she had been fervently in love with Morton Dirk. When she arrived at home, she was certain that she liked him. Two days later, after talking with her friend, she was not even sure of that. The last conversation with

Jeanette had not gone the way she had intended. She wanted her friend to understand that she had lucked out: found the most fantastic man in the world. He was smart, erudite, a sex machine, worldly, financially secure…and he could actually cook. And now, she was wasn't sure about anything. Wasn't sure she wanted him to call again. Maybe he wouldn't. And she could get back to her old life: an occasional date, occasional sex, occasional flirt. For a few more years…until the men moved on to something younger; by which time she'd be too tired for that, anyway. At least she had had a good fling with a new man. Best in her life. But…something was wrong. Something was very wrong. Something, something, something….

Then she had it: Cool. She had never seen him show annoyance or anger or excitement—just a quick smile, or a rare grin. Only once, a joke. Unruffled on the roads in Atlanta, where drivers vied to surpass the last act of incomprehensible high-speed imprudence. She remembered one occasion where he had said casually, as if he were reading a script, "We're doing about sixty-six. There's a young woman on my tail, less than a car-length away…can't even see her front lights. People like that fascinate me. It's always a surprise to look into their faces and see ordinary people. You'd expect that kind of stupidity to be related to physical peculiarities…something that indicated to the world: 'Caution. I'm an ass with a driver's licence.'"

She had found that amusing then, because she wanted him to be amusing. But now…. She had never known anyone else to speak like that. Another man would have sworn, changed lanes, or done something even more stupid—like tapping on his brake pedal. Instead, he had maintained his speed, unruffled, until the other driver swerved into another lane. And Morton had kept his gaze straight ahead, as if the other driver never existed.

Cool. Even in the middle of their lovemaking, when she had lost control of her voice, and breathing, and body; with her nails deep into the skin of his back; he had remained in control of himself—not even breathless after sex. Not even sweaty. While her own body poured and glistened and soaked his sheets.

And if he were to call tonight, she would instantly forget her concerns. She would choke over all the things she wanted to say: How she missed him. And he would say exactly the things that a distant lover should say; and make her fall in love with him all over again. Until the next night, or until she spoke to Jeanette again.

The next time he called, she would ask him: "Morton, what do you want with me?" First thing, before he said too much. Before his voice told her what to believe.

She wondered whether she should mention what Jeanette had said about his name. "Morton is the French word for death…and a dirk is a Scottish dagger. His name means death knife," Jeanette had said. Morton Dirk: Death Knife. No, that was too stupid. He had not named himself. Jeanette was a bitch. Even if she was a good friend.

She did not tell her friend how Morton turned cold when he fell asleep; how his breathing became almost imperceptible; like the diving reflex in marine mammals she had learned about: A human seal. And his hands and fingers—hard as tire treads; not like the hands of a college professor. From karate, Morton had explained.

Jeanette would have told her to change her telephone number, to move, to forget Morton, consider moving to another state. She would have given Colette the telephone numbers of every single man she knew. "Find another man, Colette. That Morton Dirk isn't the only man you can find who can give you good sex. That man ain't natural. Dump his butt. Find a man to protect you."

She would make a decision the next time he called. She was several hundred miles away, for heaven's sake. Safe. They were two adults, and she could talk to him. She would mention all the things that bothered her about him. If he didn't like it, tough. That would take care of the relationship. Had a good time; no hard feelings. Good memories. Thanks for everything.

On the other hand.... There would be Selwyn: "Like my shirt? Silk. Cost me almost a hundred bucks. Bought it just for you. Think I'm gonna change brands...too many people wearing Armani suits, now."

Or Winsell: "C'mon, baby. You know I'm good for you. A fine woman like you can't go on living alone. You wasting your life, girl...and that sweet booty. That sweet, sweet, booty."

Her regular dates: Good looks—Selwyn was beautiful. Fine entertainment—Winsell was a smooth dancer. Acceptable sex—from both...and ten minutes of vacuous conversation—on a good day. But it was better than staying home and reading Erotique Noire.

Then.... Morton arrived with the ashes of her late husband, and left her old quiet world razed and torched. She wanted Morton to bury her again with words. Wanted to see forests and oceans. Wanted him to leave her body wet, exhausted, aching...and exhilarated from his pounding. Wanted him to talk into her ear again. Send her to sleep with his whispers; hold her suspended in the air above the bed with his poetry.

It was one thirty in the morning, and she could not fall asleep. "Morton, Morton, Morton, Morton, Morton." She screamed his name into the pillow she clutched against her breast. Pulled her clothes off and reached for the telephone. Put it between her legs. Morton, Morton, Morton.

Let Jeanette...and her own better sense protest. At the first opportunity, she would tell Morton she loved him.

Less than a minute later, she fell into profound sleep with no dreams.

Morton called on Christmas night. "Still want to go to Puerto Rico?" he asked.

"Oh yes, lovey" she said. "Yes, yes, yes!"

"Sorry I didn't have time to get you a present, but when we get to San Juan...."

"Just tie a ribbon around yourself." She was shouting and crying into the telephone. "Don't want anything else. Start taking your clothes off when you get into the terminal." She had almost forgotten to ask: "When are you coming?"

"Tonight," he said. "I'm calling from the airport in Atlanta. My flight leaves in forty five minutes. Here's the flight number. I'll see you in a couple hours."

"Morton?"

"Yes?"

"No…I'll ask you when you get here. Let me go find something sexy to wear. See you later, lovey."

"Something wrong, Colette?" Morton asked.

"Nothing you aren't going to fix," she replied.

"I'm a hard worker," Morton said.

"I know. And I can be demanding."

"Yes, Ma'am….I know."

12

February fourteenth.

The call came to his office. "Dirk," the voice on the telephone said. "It's Point."

Morton frowned at the telephone. Clarence Point had never called him before, not even at home. He could hear traffic in the background—Point was calling from a pay telephone. Something very bad was about to happen.

"Yes?"

"The Organization has decided to terminate Colette Delaware."

"You?" Morton asked. His chair could no longer support him. He slid forward to kneel the floor. Gripped the edge of the desk. Tried not to panic. "You?" he repeated.

"Yes. Tomorrow night. I'm sorry."

"Why are you telling me?" Morton asked.

"Because you will come afer me. I know Queller's death wasn't an accident…he was too good. I expect to meet you in Denver. We will end it there. Goodbye, Morton Dirk."

"Goodbye, Clarence Point."

Colette's School…High School…Everton. Everton High School. Morton walked quickly out of his office, out to the parking lot. It didn't matter if he missed his next class. There would not be a next class. Goodbye Charteris, Gaynor Franklyn, Mrs. Mountrie, bread pudding, Atlanta…Judge Augustus Telamon….

He stopped at a pay telephone outside an Eckerd's pharmacy. Called information in Denver. "Everton High School, please." He followed the recorded directions, and put more coins in. Waited.

On the second ring: "Everton High School. Would you hold, please?" a woman's voice said.

"No. I can't," Morton shouted, but he had been already put on hold.

When the voice came back, he said quickly, "I must speak to Ms. Colette Delaware, please. It's very urgent."

"Ms. Delaware is in a class now, sir. Can she…?"

"No," Morton said. "This cannot wait. It's a family emergency."

"May I ask who's calling, sir?"

"Dr. Dirk," he said. "Will you hurry, please?"

The woman put the telephone down, hard. A minute later, Colette picked the handset. "Morton?" She was breathless.

"Yes. Colette, listen very, very carefully. Do not ask any questions. Understand?"

"Yes," she said.

"Try and remain calm until you get home. As soon as you get off, go to a gun store and buy a nine millimeter automatic handgun. Insist on one of the best they have. About five, six hundred dollars. I'll reimburse you. Ask them to load it for you, and to show you the safety catch. When you get home, make sure the safety is off. Remember: Off. Push the gun down between the cushion and the armrest on the right side of the couch in the living room…make sure it doesn't show. Got all of that? Good. I'm leaving in a couple hours for Denver. I'll call and leave a message on your machine with the time and flight number. I'll see you at the airport."

"Morton, what's going on? Please?" Colette was close to losing control.

Morton's voice calmed. Began to soothe. "I'll take care of you, Colette. Don't worry...I'll take care of you. And...I love you, Colette Delaware. With all my heart...I really do love you." He put the telephone down. Drove home.

Calm...calm. Think...think. Take care of Colette. It was over for him. He had expected that. But not for Colette.

He opened a safe bolted to the floor of the walk-in closet in his bedroom. Took out several documents which he put in to a slim long Manilla envelope. Put this into the inner pocket of his jacket. Put all of the cash in the safe in other pockets. One thousand, three hundred, nine dollars and seventy three cents.

Took a last look around the house, and turned the lights off. The Organization would take care of the rest. He drove to his bank and asked to close his accounts. Eleven thousand dollars. He asked for a cashier's check for the amount. Gave the name of the men's shelter. He drove to the shelter and went in to see the superintendent. Gave him the cashier's check. "I'm going away for a while, and I won't be needing the car. Here's the title, and I'll write you up a deed of sale. I'm leaving the car to the shelter. Can you call me a taxi?"

The superintendent's mouth was tight. He nodded. "You won't be coming back," he said.

In the taxi, Morton spoke Victor Hugo's poem softly to himself:

"(Demain, des l'aube)
Tomorrow, at dawn, when light whitens the countryside,
I shall leave. You see, I know you're waiting for me.
I shall come through the forest, and over the mountain.
I can no longer live far away from you.
I shall walk with my eyes fixed on my thoughts.
Seeing nothing around me, hearing no other sound,

Alone, unknown, my back bent, my hands crossed,
Sad, and the day for me will be like the night...."

The taxi driver saw the movements of his lips, and asked: "Said something, sir?"

Morton shook his head.

Five hours later, Morton walked toward the winged gargoyle above Exit 506 at Denver Airport. Colette wore a heavy black wool coat. Her eyes were red and swollen. Her lips smudged with remnants of lipstick. There were faint incrustations of dried tears down her cheeks.

In the car, Morton handed her the Manilla envelope. It contained the number of his account in the offshore Caribbean bank and the access codes. He took the cash out of his pockets and put it into her purse.

"Keep your speed down," he said, "You're doing eighty five."

"Morton, I'm so scared...I'm so scared. What's going on? I'm going to die, Morton? Tell me what's going on, Morton. Please? Why are you giving me money? What's in the envelope?"

"When we get to the house, I'll tell you everything. I promise. Everything."

She broke off the left side mirror on her car getting into the garage. Morton had to take the keys from her hand to open the kitchen door.

Clarence Point was in the living room, sitting on the chair facing the door they had just entered. A pistol with a silencer lay across his knees. One day early. Point was cautious, as Morton had expected.

Morton grabbed Colette quickly around her shoulders to stop her from falling to the floor. She was trembling uncontrollably, gasping for breath. He had to carry her to the couch facing Point's chair. Placed her on his left. Sat down beside her. "One favor," he asked Point. "Let me tell her what this is all about."

"Why?" Point asked.

"A last act of decency," Morton said.

"Go ahead. I'm early." Point shrugged.

Morton told her everything that had happened since the moment of his parents' deaths. It took him half an hour.

Point never took his eyes off the couple. No movements except for the regular blinking of his eyes and the slow heave and fall of his chest. His right hand rested on the butt of his gun, the tip of his index finger nested in the concavity of the trigger.

Morton Dirk stopped. "Done?" Point asked.

"Yes."

Point's grip tightened on the gun and it began to rise in Morton's direction.

"No!" Colette screamed, and threw herself at the gun. Morton grabbed her arm, pulled her back. Point's glance flickered toward her, then back to Morton. Found himself looking into the barrel of a pistol. Saw the yellow flash just before the air shook with thunder. The bullet kicked him in the left shoulder. He fired twice at Morton before his body had stopped moving. Morton's gun roared again, and Point's right cheek and nose disintegrated. As Point fought to steady his gun, Morton fired into his chest. Point fell to his knees. Fired again. A dark spot appeared in Morton's right chest. Both men lay on their backs on the floor, struggling to rise. There was blood everywhere; and the air was fogged with blue smoke. Morton rolled his body toward Point, pushing against the leg of the couch with his right elbow.

The other man had turned to lie on his stomach; his breath gurgled through the blood pouring out through the remnants of his mouth and cheek. The rest of his face remained calm, his eyes focused on the completion of his mission. He willed his body to postpone its dying.

Morton lay on his left side, his right hand fighting the weight of the gun. He reached with his left hand to support the weapon. Point was rising from the floor. Morton tried to fire, but the trigger was too hard to pull. He managed to level the gun although both hands trembled violently. Concentrated on the mechanism of the gun. The pistol steadied. Point was staggering toward him. Morton's finger tightened on the trigger. It seemed to take minutes: he saw the hammer rise, waver, then fall slowly against the firing pin; saw the pin dent the cap, saw the mercury fulminate flash and ignite the cordite. An orange star stretched into a tongue and flung the lead slug ahead of its tip. The rifling in the barrel caught the lead and spun it. It came out of the barrel revolving on its long axis. Flame and smoke followed, and the room twisted with the roar of the expanding gases. The slug flew toward Point, who was diving strait at it. They met when Point was three feet away from Morton. The bullet entered his sternal notch, taking away his throat, and slapping his head back. His mouth and lacerated cheek were open in a wide grin as he collapsed. It was the first time that Morton Dirk had seen amusement on the face of Clarence Point. His own ears were ringing from the gunshots, and there was another growing sound, coming from a great drum inside his chest, threatening to burst through his ribs. As if his heart were beating its funeral march.

Colette rose slowly from the floor beside the couch where she had been kneeling, with her hands over her ears. Morton was writhing on the ground, his fingers pressed against his chest and abdomen. "No ambulance…tell the police I tried to protect you…from an intruder. Call Telamon…I'll give you his number. Tell him you belong to the Organization. You'll have to do whatever they want…or they'll kill you…can never get away from them, now…never."

"What? Morton what are you saying?"

"Tell him…please…he'll understand…be brave…now…. Call."

Colette went to the telephone. Dialed the digits Morton called out slowly.

"Telamon," a deep male voice said.

"Judge Telamon, my name is Colette Delaware. Morton Dirk is dying. Clarence Point is dead."

Silence.

"Sir?" she said.

"What do you want?" Telamon asked.

"I belong to the Organization, now," she said.

"Please explain," Telamon said.

"My death would be of no use to you. My life will be a small compensation for your losses. I am a teacher. A good teacher...like Morton. I teach science."

"What can you do for the Organization?"

"I am a quick learner...I'm sure there is something I can do well for the Organization."

"What did Morton tell you about this 'Organization?'" Telamon asked.

"Everything...from the time his parents died."

"And you believe you can handle that?"

"Rather than die...yes," she said.

"I know nothing about you."

"Judge Telamon, I believe you know everything about me. From what Morton...."

Telamon interrupted her. "If I employ you, it will be because of Morton. But remember...you will be of limited value to us...and if you became more of a problem than an asset, we would have to let you go."

"Get rid of me."

"Let you go," he repeated. "I am sure you understand."

"Perfectly," she said.

"You will have to come to Atlanta...and you will lose much of your freedom. You understand?"

"I understand."

"But you would be well provided for. And...I believe Morton has seen to that."

"He gave me an envelope, I haven't opened it," Colette said.

"In that envelope are instructions giving you complete access to his bank accounts. You are a rich woman."

"Oh, God. I don't want his money."

"I am sure that you will find a way to deal with that dilemma in time," Telamon said.

"I have to go back to Morton now…and I have to call the police. I'm going to have a lot of explaining to do when they get here. They may want me to remain in Denver indefinitely."

"I'll take care of that," Telamon said.

"How do I know you people won't try to kill me?" Colette asked.

"Your death would be of no use to me," Telamon replied.

She put the telephone down and went back to Morton. He lay on his back. Opened his eyes slightly. Tried to focus on her face. "Did you love me, Colette Delaware?" he asked. It took him several seconds to get the words out.

She knelt beside him and took his right hand. Held it tight between her breasts. "With all my heart, Morton Dirk. Still…lovey," she said, and kissed his mouth.

"Did Telamon agree?"

"Yes."

"Good," he said, and closed his eyes. The pain in his body made him feel that he had been inserted into a furnace. But it abated when he focused his mind on the recollection of Colette's face. Lovey. Such a beautiful word…he had never heard it before. Lovey. Lovey. Lovey. He listened to the word echo around his mind. Tried to pull more of her perfume into his lungs, but the weight pressing down on his chest was too much. It was pushing him through the floor and into the earth below the house. He was hurtling down a steep river; could not move his arms or legs; did not feel any pain when he brushed against rocks on the banks or on the river bed. He lay on his back in the water but the spray of water on his face did not trouble him—he did not have to breathe if he did not want to. He wanted to assure Colette that dying was not as terrifying as he had imagined…at least, it eased the pain. And the pain was going away…out of his chest and up his arm…into the fingers wrapped tightly around his hand. So soft. He could not remember whether he had told her he loved her. Perhaps he should tell her again. "Colette?" he called. "Colette?" But he did not hear her reply.

In Atlanta, Telamon sat at his desk with his head in his hands, staring at the telephone near his left hand. He did not move for an hour. Finally he straightened, dabbed his eyes on his sleeve, and picked up the telephone. Dialed. He let it ring three times then pressed the release button. Waited a few seconds and dialed again. After the fourth ring, a voice slightly distorted by the descrambler said: "Yes?"

"Georgia?"

"Yes, Judge."

"Morton's dead...and Point. Killed each other in Denver. Colette Delaware survived."

Georgia Enoch did not answer. Telamon heard the quick intake of breath and the long sigh. "I'm very sorry, Georgia. I loved him too."

"It's his son, Judge. All these years...wondering what it was going to be like when they met each other."

"I'll be happy to take care of him. Do you want to send him to Atlanta?"

"No. He's too much like his father. I want his life to be different."

"He belongs to...to the Organization, Georgia. But I understand. We'll work that out. Now, about Ms. Delaware. She called—Morton made her...before he died. Wants to join the Organization."

"What does she know about the Organization?"

"Apparently Morton had time to tell her quite enough. We may be able to use her. She's had an aseptic life. Nothing to hold against her. Would you be willing to handle her?"

"Do I have a choice? Will she be eliminated"

"No, enough dying for the moment. You don't have much choice really, but I would rather you agreed to do it. She doesn't have to like you, but she will have to respect you."

"About my son," Georgia said.

"You'll be with him...there's not much we can expect from him. The boy will be safe."

"When will you want me?"

"In about a week..."

"Yes, sir. Will Colette Delaware learn about Morton's son?"
"What do you want?"
"I would rather that she did not."
"As you wish. But that's no guarantee that she won't suspect it."
"Thank you, Judge."
"Thank you. Goodbye, Georgia."

Telamon rose and paced about his room for twenty minutes, then picked up the telephone again. A voice answered: "Reason for your call?"

"John Milton," Telamon replied.

A pause, then another voice asked: "Paradise Lost?" It sounded like dry leaves being crushed underfoot.

"Paradise Regained," said Judge Augustus Telamon.

"Name?"

"Colette Delaware, Denver."

"Ah." Then the voice was silent for what seemed several minutes. Telamon did not break the silence. Kept his breathing quiet.

"And you have thoroughly considered the risk?" the voice asked.

"From this moment, we know everything she says and does. At the slightest suspicion, we will remove her. Of course, she will be in quarantine in Atlanta…for two years. But we don't have anyone like her."

Finally, the voice rustled again—dry leaves blowing down a freezing dark ancient corridor: "Yes…and Miss. Enoch was a prostitute…but has been a great asset. Do you have a control for Colette Delaware?"

"Yes," Telamon replied, "Georgia Enoch."

"Bring in Colette Delaware," the voice said; and Telamon was left with the dial tone.

ABOUT THE AUTHOR

Earl Long is a graduate of the London University, School of Tropical Medicine. His two previous novels, "Consolation" and "Voices from a Drum" were published by Addison-Wesley Longman, and he was the first-prize winner of the 1993 Essence Magazine Short Story Competition. He lives and works in Atlanta, Georgia.